This book
belongs to:

_____

_____

Bedtime Stories

Sleepytime tales to share

This edition published by Parragon Books Ltd in 2016

Parragon Books Ltd
Chartist House
15–17 Trim Street
Bath BA1 1HA, UK
www.parragon.com

ISBN 978-1-4748-2089-9

Printed in China

Bedtime Stories

Sleepytime tales to share

PaRRagon

Bath • New York • Cologne • Melbourne • Delhi
Hong Kong • Shenzhen • Singapore • Amsterdam

Contents

Jack and the Beanstalk

There was once a young boy called Jack, who lived with his mother. They had no money and nothing left to eat.

"We have no choice but to sell Bluebell, our old cow," said Jack's mother. "Take her to market and sell her for a good price."

So Jack set off with Bluebell.

Before long, he met an old man, who asked, "Are you selling that fine cow?"

"Yes," Jack replied.

"Well, I'll give you these magic beans for her," said the man. "They don't look much, but if you plant them, you will soon be rich!"

Jack liked the sound of that and he gave Bluebell to the man.

When Jack showed his mother the beans, she was very angry.

"Silly boy! Go to your room!" she cried, throwing the beans out of the window.

The next morning, when Jack woke up, his room was strangely dark. He looked out of his window and saw a plant so tall that he couldn't see the top of it.

"It must be a magic beanstalk!" he cried.

Jack started to climb. When he reached the top, he saw a giant house. Jack's tummy was rumbling with hunger, so he knocked on the enormous door and a giant woman answered.

"Please may I have some breakfast?" asked Jack.

"You'll BE breakfast if my husband sees you!" said the woman.

But Jack begged and pleaded, and at last the giant's wife let him in. She gave him some bread and milk, and hid him in a cupboard.

Soon, Jack heard loud footsteps and felt the cupboard shake.

"Fee-fi-fo-fum! I smell the blood of an Englishman!" roared the giant.

"Don't be silly," the giant's wife said. "You smell the sausages I've cooked for your breakfast."

When the giant had finished eating, he counted the hundreds of huge gold coins in his treasure chest. But the counting soon sent him to sleep.

As quick as a flash, Jack grabbed the coins, ran out of the house and climbed down the beanstalk.

His mother was so happy to see the gold. "Clever boy! We'll never be poor again!" she laughed.

But soon Jack and his mother had spent all the money, so the boy climbed the beanstalk again. He knocked on the huge door and begged the giant's wife to give him some food. At last, she let him in.

After eating his breakfast, Jack hid in the cupboard, just as the giant arrived home for lunch.

When the giant had finished eating, his wife brought him his pet hen.

"Lay!" he bellowed, and the hen laid a golden egg. It laid ten eggs before the giant started to snore. Jack couldn't believe his luck, so he picked up the hen and ran.

His mother beamed when she saw the hen lay a golden egg.

"We will never be hungry again!" she said.

But even though Jack and his mother were now rich, the boy decided to climb the beanstalk one more time.

Jack knew the giant's wife wouldn't be happy to see him, so he sneaked in when she wasn't looking and hid in the cupboard.

When the giant came home, his wife brought him his magic harp.

"Play!" he roared, and the harp played such sweet music that the giant soon fell asleep.

Jack saw his chance and grabbed the harp. As he ran, the harp cried out, "Master! Help!"

The giant woke up and began to chase Jack down the beanstalk.

"Mother, fetch the axe!" Jack yelled as he reached the ground. He chopped at the beanstalk with all his might. CREAK! GROAN! The giant quickly climbed back to the top just before the beanstalk crashed to the ground.

When his mother heard the harp play, she laughed and hugged Jack tightly.

"My clever boy!" she said. And the two of them lived happily ever after.

Little Red Riding Hood

There was once a sweet little girl who always wore a lovely red cape with a hood. Everyone called her Little Red Riding Hood.

"Granny is poorly," said her mother one morning. "Take her this basket of food and don't talk to any strangers!"

So Little Red Riding Hood took the basket and set off right away.

Very soon, she met a wolf.

"Hello," said the wolf. "Where are you going?"

"I'm visiting my poorly granny," replied Little Red Riding Hood, forgetting her mother's warning. "She lives on the other side of this wood."

While Little Red Riding Hood picked some flowers for Granny, the wolf raced down the path to the old lady's cottage.

He opened the door, and before Granny had a chance to shout for help, the wicked creature opened his huge jaws and swallowed her whole! Then he climbed into her bed, pulled the covers up under his chin and waited.

Soon, Little Red Riding Hood reached Granny's house, with her basket of food and posy of flowers.

When she went into the bedroom, she gasped in surprise. Her granny didn't look well at all!

"Granny," she exclaimed. "Your ears are enormous!"

"All the better to hear you with," growled the wolf.

"And your eyes are as big as saucers," she gulped.

"All the better to see you with," snarled the wolf.

"And your teeth are so…pointed!" she gasped.

"All the better to EAT you with!" roared the wolf, and he swallowed Little Red Riding Hood in one GULP! Then he fell fast asleep.

Luckily, a nearby woodcutter heard some loud snoring sounds coming from the cottage.

He tiptoed inside and found the sleeping wolf…with his tummy bulging.

The woodcutter tipped the wolf upside-down and shook him hard. Out fell Little Red Riding Hood and out fell Granny!

Granny was so furious, she chased the wolf far into the wood and they never saw him again!

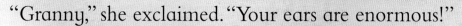

Want to Swap?

It was bedtime, but Duck couldn't sleep. "I'm bored of being a duck and nibbling waterweeds," she said to herself.

Then she saw her friend Cockerel strolling around the pond and had a brilliant idea.

"Hey, Cockerel," she called. "Want to swap jobs?"

"Okay," Cockerel agreed. "Nibbling waterweeds is better than getting up early every day."

So, the next morning, Duck waddled to the farmhouse for her first cock-a-doodle-do to wake the farmer up. But when she opened her beak…

"Quack! Quack! QUACK!"

Poor Duck! However hard she tried, she couldn't crow, and the farmer overslept.

"I want my old job back," Duck said sadly.

Luckily for Duck, Cockerel was not enjoying his new job much either.

"Waterweeds are yucky and I kind of missed waking the farmer up," he said.

The next day, when Duck saw Sheepdog herding sheep, she had a thought. She waddled up to the field.

"That looks like fun, Sheepdog," she said. "Want to swap?"

Sheep's Bad Mood

Sheep was in a bad mood. His friends on the farm tried to cheer him up, but their jokes didn't help. Sheep just felt as if there were a growly bear inside him trying to get out.

"I've an idea," said Horse, who was very clever about this sort of thing. "Try doing some hard work."

"How can hard work help?" Sheep grumbled. But no one had any better ideas, so Sheep decided to give it a try. He carried baskets of eggs for the chickens. He lifted bales of hay for the horses. He rode in the tractor with the farmer. He worked so hard that he started to forget about his bad mood. And at bedtime, when all the weary farm animals snuggled down in the barn, Horse noticed that Sheep was smiling.

"Has it gone?" asked Horse.

"Has what gone?" yawned Sheep.

"Your bad mood," said Horse, chuckling loudly.

But there was no reply. Sheep was already fast asleep!

Bunny Loves to Learn

One morning, Buster Bunny and his best friends, Sam the squirrel, Max the mouse and Francine the frog, arrived at school.

"What's in those boxes, Miss?" asked Buster.

"Costumes!" said Miss Nibbler. "Today, you're going to dress up as people who lived a long time ago. I want you to make something from the time when they lived and tell us all about it!"

"I'm going to find out about Vikings," said Buster.

"I want to be a knight," said Sam. "They have amazing helmets!"

"I think I'll be a princess!" cried Francine.

"I can't decide what to find out about," said Max.

"Why don't you dress up as an Egyptian ruler?" said Buster, taking a book from the shelf. "They were called pharaohs."

But the pharaoh's crown was missing from the box.

"I don't want to be a king without a crown!" said Max.

Just then, he noticed a poster on the classroom wall.

"I want to be an Egyptian mummy!" he said. "They're so cool!"

He rummaged in the costume box.

"Bother," he said. "There's no mummy costume."

"I've got a knight's sword and helmet," said Sam. "I'm going to make a shield to go with them."

"I'm building a model of a Viking ship," said Buster.

"And I'm making a palace for a princess," said Francine.

Soon, Buster, Sam and Francine were busy making things. But Max still didn't know what to make.

"I really want to dress as a mummy," he grumbled.

"What else do you know about Egyptians?" asked Buster.

"I know they built big pyramids," said Max.

"Why don't you build one of those?" suggested Buster.

Max found some big sheets of card and tried to make a pyramid.

"Oh dear," he said. "This is trickier than I thought."

Francine showed him how to look up pyramids on the computer.

"Ah, now I see," said Max. "A pyramid has four sides, not three. And each side is exactly the same size."

Max finished his pyramid proudly, but then he sighed. "I still don't know what to wear!" he said.

15

"Ouch!" said Buster suddenly. "I just got a paper cut!"

"It's only a small one," said Miss Nibbler. "But you'd better nip to the school nurse for a plaster."

"That gives me an idea!" said Buster. He whispered in Max's ear.

"Brilliant!" laughed Max. "Please don't be long!"

When it was time to present to the class, the friends took it in turns to show what they had made.

"I'm a knight," said Sam. "My shield protected me in battle. It was brightly painted so that my friends could recognize me when my helmet was shut!"

"I'm a princess," said Francine. "I lived in a palace. I wore long silky dresses and tall pointy hats. And I often got to boss around all the knights!"

Buster, back from the nurse, showed the class his Viking ship. "I'm a Viking," he said. "I loved to sail in a very fast ship called a longship. It had a dragon's head carved on the front to scare my enemies!"

"Thanks, Buster," said Miss Nibbler. "Now it's Max's turn."

"Egyptians lived a very, very long time ago," said a voice. But Max was nowhere to be seen…

"They built amazing pyramids," the voice went on. "The pyramids were taller than ten houses on top of each other! Nobody lived in them, except for – MUMMIES! RAAAAH!"

And Max leaped out of the pyramid.

"So that's where you were hiding!" cried Francine.

"Where did you get that brilliant mummy costume?" asked Sam. "I thought there wasn't one."

"I borrowed the bandages from the school nurse," said Max. "It was Buster's idea."

"Clever thinking, Buster!" said Miss Nibbler. "And well done to everybody. Your costumes look amazing and you've all learned some really interesting things. What a wonderful show and tell!"

How the Leopard Got Its Spots

Long ago, Leopard lived on a sandy-yellow plain in Africa. Giraffes and zebras and deer lived there too. The animals were sandy-yellow all over, just like the plain itself. Leopard was sandy-yellow, too, which wasn't good for the rest of the animals because he could hide in the sandy-yellow grasses, then jump out and eat them.

After a while, the other animals had had enough. They decided to move away from the sandy plain into the forest. In the forest, the sun shone through the trees, making stripy, spotty and patchy shadows on the ground.

The animals hid themselves there, and while they hid, their skins changed colour, becoming stripy, spotty and patchy too.

Meanwhile, Leopard was hungry.

"Where has everyone gone?" he asked Baboon.

"To the forest," said Baboon carelessly, "to hide from you!"

Leopard decided to go to the forest to hunt for his dinner.
But when he got there, all he could see were tree trunks. They
were stripy, spotty and patchy with shadows. He couldn't see
the other animals, but he could smell them, so he knew they
were there.

Meanwhile, the other animals could easily spot the
sandy-yellow leopard in the forest, so they stayed hidden away.

Hungry and tired, Leopard lay down in a spotty shadow to rest.
After a while, he noticed he wasn't sandy-yellow any more.
He had small, dark spots on his skin, just like the spotty shadow
he was lying in.

"Aha!" he thought. "Giraffe and Zebra and the other animals
must have changed their skin colour. But now my skin is no
longer sandy-yellow, I can hide too. Then, when they come close,
I can leap out and eat them up!"

With that, the spotty leopard set off into the shadowy forest to
eat, sleep and NOT be spotted. And the other animals learned to
hide from him as best they could, too!

A Nutty Adventure

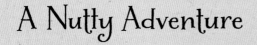

Squirrel was scurrying around the forest floor, gathering nuts ready for winter. Then, when he was sure nobody was looking, he pushed them, one by one, into his secret hidey-hole at the bottom of the giant beech tree.

It was hard work and soon Squirrel needed a break. He peeped into the hole to see how many nuts he had collected.

But the hidey-hole was empty!

Squirrel was so angry that he stamped his feet and squeaked at the top of his voice, "Someone's stolen my pile of nuts!"

Rabbit hopped over to her friend, rubbing her head.

"Well, someone has been dropping nuts on me," she cried. "I've just had to sweep them all out of my house."

Rabbit began to laugh. She had realized what had happened. Squirrel had been pushing the nuts through her window!

When Rabbit explained, Squirrel began to chuckle too.

"What a nutty adventure!" he laughed.

The Egg

Little Parrot lived in a nest with Mummy and a big pink speckled egg.

"I'm going to find some food," Mummy told Little Parrot one day. "You must look after the egg until I return."

Little Parrot watched the egg for a very long time.

Then, she wobbled it around to make it comfortable and wrapped her wings around it to keep it warm.

"I'm very good at looking after eggs," she squawked, feeling pleased with herself.

Just then, Little Parrot heard a tap, tap, tapping noise coming from the egg, then…CRACK!

"Oh, no, I've broken it!" she cried. "Mummy will be cross!"

But when Mummy returned, she wasn't angry at all.

"Look," she said, as a tiny baby parrot popped out of the broken eggshell. "You took care of the egg perfectly. Now it's hatched and you've got a new baby sister to play with!"

Goldilocks and the
Three Bears

Once upon a time, there was a little girl called
Goldilocks who had beautiful golden hair. She lived in
a little cottage right at the edge of the forest.

One morning, before breakfast, Goldilocks skipped into the
forest to play. She soon strayed far from home and began
to feel hungry.

Just as she was thinking about going home, a delicious
smell wafted through the wood. She followed it all the way
to a little cottage.

"I wonder who lives here?" thought Goldilocks. She knocked
on the door, but there was no answer.

As Goldilocks pushed gently on the door, it swung open, and
Goldilocks stepped inside.

The delicious smell was coming from three bowls of steaming porridge on a table. There was a great big bowl, a middle-sized bowl and a teeny-tiny bowl.

Goldilocks was so hungry, she tried the porridge in the biggest bowl first.

"Ooh! Too hot!" she cried.

Next, she tasted the porridge in the middle-sized bowl.

"Yuck! Too cold!" she spluttered.

So Goldilocks tried the porridge in the teeny-tiny bowl.

"Yum," she said. "Just right." And she ate it all up.

Goldilocks saw three comfy chairs by the fire. There was a great big chair, a middle-sized chair and a teeny-tiny chair.

"Just the place for a nap," yawned Goldilocks sleepily.

She tried to scramble onto the biggest chair. "Too high up!" she gasped, sliding to the ground.

Next, Goldilocks tried the middle-sized chair, but she sank into the cushions. "Too squishy!" she grumbled.

So Goldilocks tried the teeny-tiny chair. "Just right," she sighed, settling down. But Goldilocks was full of porridge and too heavy for the teeny-tiny chair. It squeaked and creaked, creaked and cracked. Then…CRASH!

It broke into teeny-tiny pieces and Goldilocks fell to the floor.

"Ouch!" she said.

Goldilocks climbed up the stairs. At the top, she found a bedroom with three beds. There was a great big bed, a middle-sized bed and a teeny-tiny bed.

"I'll just lie down for a while," yawned Goldilocks. So she clambered onto the biggest bed. "Too hard!" she grumbled.

Then, she lay down on the middle-sized bed. "Too soft!" she mumbled.

So she snuggled down in the teeny-tiny bed. "Just right," she sighed, and fell fast asleep.

Meanwhile, a great big daddy bear, a middle-sized mummy bear and a teeny-tiny baby bear returned home from their walk in the woods.

"The porridge should be cool enough to eat now," said Mummy Bear.

So the three bears went inside their cottage for breakfast.

"Someone's been eating my porridge!" growled Daddy Bear, looking in his bowl.

"Someone's been eating my porridge!" gasped Mummy Bear, looking in her bowl.

"Someone's been eating my porridge," squeaked Baby Bear, "and they've eaten it all up!"

Then, Daddy Bear went over to his chair.

"Someone's been sitting in my chair," he roared. "There's a golden hair on it!'"

"Someone's been sitting in my chair," growled Mummy Bear. "The cushions are all squashed!"

"Someone's been sitting in my chair," cried Baby Bear, "and they've broken it!"

The three bears stomped upstairs.

Daddy Bear looked at his crumpled bed covers.

"Someone's been sleeping in my bed!" he grumbled.

Mummy Bear looked at the jumbled pillows on her bed.

"Someone's been sleeping in my bed!" she said.

Baby Bear padded over to his bed.

"Someone's been sleeping in my bed," he cried, "and they're still there!"

At that moment, Goldilocks woke up. When she saw the three bears, she leaped out of the bed, ran down the stairs, through the door, into the woods and all the way home! And she never visited the house of the three bears ever again.

I Love My Mummy

One morning, Little Deer didn't want to play in his garden any more.

"I want to see new things," he told his mummy.

"Then let's go exploring," said Mummy Deer.

"This way!" cried Little Deer excitedly.

When Little Deer came to the stream, he slowly crossed the wobbly stones, watching the water as it trickled gently beside him.

"Don't get your feet wet," warned Mummy.

"I won't!" said Little Deer, as he wiggled and wobbled.

On the other side of the stream, Little Deer squeezed through the tangly bushes.

"Don't get stuck," warned Mummy.

"I won't! Hurry up, Mummy!" said Little Deer. "Look! A hill that goes up to the clouds!"

Little Deer climbed all the way to the top, panting with each step.

"I can see forever!" cried Little Deer, wobbling as he stood on tiptoes.

Then suddenly…

"Wheeee!" cried Little Deer, as he slid down the other side of the hill into a meadow.

"Are you okay?" asked his mummy.

"Yes!" giggled Little Deer. "I am!"

Little Deer looked around the meadow. "Mummy?" he said anxiously. "Which way is home? I'm lost!"

"We'll soon find our way back," Mummy Deer said soothingly. "We just have to remember how we got here."

Little Deer thought and thought. At last, he began to remember.

"We came over the hill!" said Little Deer, and he scampered back up the hill. "I can see the way from here!"

Little Deer and his mummy skidded down the other side of the hill. "We squeezed through those tangly bushes!" cried Little Deer, and they pushed through them.

"Which way now?" said Mummy Deer.

Little Deer heard the tinkling sound of a stream.

"The wobbly stones!" cheered Little Deer. "Don't get your feet wet, Mummy!"

"I won't!" laughed Mummy Deer.

Little Deer knew the way from here. He ran as fast as he could, until he reached his garden.

"I love exploring," cried Little Deer happily. "And I love my mummy!"

The Swallow and the Crow

One day, a young swallow landed on a branch next to a wise old crow. The swallow looked down his beak at the crow and said, "I don't think much of your stiff feathers. You should take more pride in your appearance."

The old crow was very angry and was about to fly away, when the swallow continued, "Look at me with my soft, downy feathers. They are what a well-dressed bird needs."

"Those soft feathers of yours might be all right in the spring and summer," the crow replied, "but in the winter you have to fly away to warmer countries. In the winter, the trees are covered in ripe berries. I can stay here and enjoy them because I have my stiff, black feathers to keep me warm and dry."

The crow held out his wings. "What use are your fancy feathers then, Swallow?" he asked, before turning away.

And the moral of the story is: fine-weather friends are not worth much.

The Dog and His Reflection

A hungry dog passed a butcher's shop and spotted a juicy steak lying on the counter. He waited until the butcher went to the back of the shop, then he ran in and stole it.

On his way home, the dog crossed a narrow bridge over a river. As he looked down into the water, he saw another dog looking up at him. This dog was also carrying a piece of meat and it looked even bigger than the one he had!

"I want that steak too," thought the greedy dog. So he jumped into the river to steal the steak from the other dog.

But, as he opened his mouth to snatch the steak, the butcher's steak fell from the dog's mouth and sank to the bottom of the river. The other dog vanished in a pool of ripples.

The greedy dog had been fooled by his own reflection, and now he was still hungry and had nothing left to eat!

And the moral of the story is: it doesn't pay to be greedy.

The Frog Prince

Long ago, a princess lived with her father in a palace surrounded by woods.

When it was hot outside, the princess would walk into the shade of the forest and sit by a pond. There, she would play with her favourite toy, a golden ball.

One day, the ball slipped from her hand and fell to the bottom of the pond. "My beautiful golden ball!" she sobbed.

An ugly, speckled frog popped his head out of the water. "Why are you crying?" he croaked.

"I've dropped my precious golden ball into the water," cried the princess.

"What will you give me if I get it for you?" asked the frog.

"You may have my jewels," sobbed the unhappy princess.

"I don't need those," said the frog. "If you promise to care for me and be my friend, let me share food from your plate and sleep on your pillow, then I will bring back your golden ball."

"I promise," said the princess, but she thought to herself, "He's only a silly old frog. I won't do any of those things."

When the frog returned with the ball, she snatched it from him and ran back to the palace.

That evening, the princess was having dinner with her father when there was a knock on the door.

When the princess opened the door, she was horrified to find the frog sitting there. She slammed the door and hurried back to the table.

"Who was that?" asked the king.

"Oh, just a frog," replied the princess.

"What does a frog want with you?" asked the puzzled king.

The princess told her father about the promise she had made. "Princesses always keep their promises," insisted the king. "Let the frog in and make him welcome."

As soon as the frog hopped through the door, he asked to be lifted up onto the princess's plate. When the frog saw the look of disgust on the princess's face, he sang:

"Princess, princess, fair and sweet, you made a special vow
To be my friend and share your food, so don't forget it now."

The king was annoyed to see his daughter acting so rudely. "This frog helped you," he said, "and now you must keep your promise to him."

For the rest of the day, the frog followed the princess everywhere she went. She hoped that he would go back to his pond when it was time for bed, but when darkness fell, the frog yawned and said, "I am tired. Take me to your room and let me sleep on your pillow."

The princess was horrified. "No, I won't!" she said rudely. "Go back to your pond and leave me alone!"

The patient frog sang:

"Princess, princess, fair and sweet, you made a special vow
To be my friend and share your food, so don't forget it now."

Reluctantly, the princess took the frog to her room. She couldn't bear the thought of sleeping next to him, so she put him on the floor. Then, she climbed into her bed and went to sleep.

After a while, the frog jumped up onto the bed. "It's draughty on the floor. Let me sleep on your pillow," he said.

The sleepy princess felt more annoyed than ever. She picked up the frog and hurled him across the room. But when she saw him lying dazed and helpless on the floor, she was suddenly filled with pity.

"Oh, you poor darling!" she cried, and she picked him up and kissed him.

Suddenly, the frog transformed into a handsome young prince.

"Sweet princess," he cried. "I was bewitched and your tender kiss has broken the curse!"

The prince and princess soon fell in love and were married. They often walked in the shady forest together and sat by the pond, tossing the golden ball back and forth, and smiling at how they first met.

Tom Thumb

There was once a poor couple who had no children and longed for a son of their own.

One day, an old beggar man passed by their house. Although the poor couple had little enough for themselves, they invited him in to eat and rest.

"Where are your children?" asked the beggar.

"We don't have any," sighed the man. "We would dearly love a son, even if he were no bigger than my thumb."

Little did the unhappy couple realize that their guest had magical powers. He rewarded their kindness by granting their wish to have a son, even a very tiny one.

The next morning, when the couple came downstairs to breakfast, they found a tiny boy waiting for them on the table. He was no bigger than the man's thumb and so his delighted parents named him Tom Thumb. Tom had an unstoppable sense of adventure. "You are only small and the world is a dangerous place," warned his mother.

But Tom was too busy having fun to listen.

One day, Tom was playing by the river. He fell in and got eaten by a fish. The fish was caught and taken to the king's chef. Being a quick-thinking lad, Tom managed to crawl out of the fish. The chef was very shocked to see a tiny boy climbing out from the king's dinner!

Thinking the chef might harm him, Tom ran away. He hid in a mouse hole and soon made friends with the mouse who lived there.

"Climb onto my back," said the mouse. And Tom rode through the palace on the mouse's back, until he found himself in the throne room.

"My goodness!" exclaimed the king. "What have we here?"

Tom sang a song and danced for the king, who was delighted with the tiny boy, and asked him to come and live at the palace.

When the king heard that Tom had parents who would be missing him, he sent for the poor couple and let them live in a cottage of their own in the royal grounds.

Tom entertained the king and all his courtiers, and he could visit his parents whenever he liked.

Tom and his parents lived happily ever after.

The Ant and the Dove

One morning, a thirsty ant went down to the river for a drink. Suddenly…SWOOSH! A ripple swept the tiny ant off the riverbank and into the water.

"Help!" cried the ant.

A kind dove heard the ant's cries. She swooped down and dropped a leaf into the water near him.

"Climb onto this," she cooed.

"Oh, thank you," gasped the ant. "You saved my life!" And he floated back to the shore on the leaf.

A little later, the ant was drying off in the sun when he saw a hunter trying to catch the dove with a net.

The ant wanted to help his new friend, so he scurried over to the hunter and bit his foot.

"Ouch!" yelled the hunter.

Startled by the noise, the dove flew away.

"Thank you," she called out to the ant. "Now you've saved my life, too!"

And the moral of the story is: one good turn deserves another.

36

The Fox and the Grapes

One hot summer's day, a fox was walking through a field when he saw a bunch of grapes dangling high above his head.

"I'm so thirsty," the fox said to himself.

"I wish I could have those juicy grapes."

Standing on his back legs, the fox stretched his neck up as far as he could, but the grapes were too high for him to reach.

Then, he took several steps backwards, ran towards the grapevine, took a giant leap and…missed!

Determined to get the delicious grapes, the fox ran and jumped, over and over again. Now, he was even hotter and thirstier than before, and he still hadn't managed to reach a single grape!

Fed up, the fox stopped jumping. Then, he stuck his pointy nose high in the air and trotted away.

"What's all the fuss about grapes, anyway?" he sniffed. "I much prefer strawberries!"

And the moral of the story is: if someone can't get something, they pretend it is not worth having.

Cinderella

Once upon a time, there was a young girl who lived with her father, stepmother and two stepsisters. The stepmother was unkind and the stepsisters were mean. They made the girl do all the housework, eat scraps, and sleep by the fireplace among the cinders and ashes. Because she was always covered in cinders, they called her Cinderella.

One morning, a special invitation arrived. All the young women in the kingdom were invited to a royal ball, so that the prince could choose a bride!

Cinderella longed to go, but her stepsisters just laughed.

"You? Go to a ball? In those rags? How ridiculous!" they cackled.

Instead, Cinderella had to rush around helping her stepsisters get ready for the ball.

As they left for the palace, Cinderella sat beside the fireplace and wept.

"I wish I could go to the ball," she cried.

Suddenly, a sparkle of light filled the dull kitchen and there was – a fairy!

"Don't be afraid, my dear," she said. "I am your fairy godmother and you SHALL go to the ball!"

"But how?" said Cinderella.

"Find me a big pumpkin, four white mice and a rat," replied the fairy godmother.

Cinderella found everything as quickly as she could. The fairy godmother waved her wand, and the pumpkin changed into a magnificent golden coach, the white mice became white horses and the rat became a coachman.

With one last gentle tap of her wand, the fairy godmother changed Cinderella's dusty dress into a shimmering ball gown. On her feet were two sparkling glass slippers.

"Now, off you go," said the fairy godmother, "but remember, all this will vanish at midnight, so make sure you are home by then."

Cinderella climbed into the coach and it whisked her away to the palace.

Everyone was enchanted by the lovely stranger, especially the prince, who danced with her all evening. As Cinderella whirled round the room in his arms, she felt so happy that she completely forgot her fairy godmother's warning.

Suddenly, she heard the clock strike midnight.

BONG...BONG...BONG...

Cinderella picked up her
skirt and fled from the
ballroom. The worried
prince ran after her.

BONG…BONG…BONG…

She ran down the palace steps, losing
a glass slipper on the way,
but she didn't dare stop.

BONG…BONG…BONG…

Cinderella jumped into the
coach and it drove off before
the prince could stop her.

BONG…BONG…BONG!

On the final stroke of midnight,
Cinderella found herself sitting
on the road beside a pumpkin, four white mice and a black
rat. She was dressed in rags and had only a single glass slipper
left from her magical evening.

At the palace, the prince saw something twinkling on the
steps – a single glass slipper.

"I will marry the woman whose foot fits this glass slipper,"
he declared.

The next day, the prince took the glass slipper and visited every house in the kingdom.

At last, the prince came to Cinderella's house. Her stepsisters tried and tried to squeeze their huge feet into the delicate slipper, but no matter what they did, they could not get the slipper to fit. Cinderella watched as she scrubbed the floor.

"May I try, please?" she asked.

"You didn't even go to the ball!" laughed the eldest stepsister.

"Everyone may try," said the prince, as he held out the sparkling slipper. And suddenly…

"Oh!" gasped the stepsisters, as Cinderella's dainty foot slipped into it easily.

The prince joyfully took Cinderella in his arms.

"Will you marry me?" he asked.

"I will!" Cinderella said.

Much to the disgust of her stepmother and stepsisters, Cinderella and the prince were soon married.

They lived long, happy lives together, and Cinderella's stepmother and daughters had to do their own cleaning, and never went to a royal ball again.

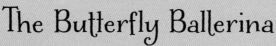

The Butterfly Ballerina

Isabella Ballerina loved ballet. Best of all, she liked going to Madame Colette's Ballet School.

"Let us practise our ballet positions!" called Madame Colette one morning, clapping her hands. "No, no, Isabella! You are pointing the wrong foot again!"

"Sorry!" Isabella said. "I'm always getting my left and right mixed up!"

"Now, girls," cried Madame Colette. "I have exciting news to announce! We will be putting on our first show: the Butterfly Ballet. I will choose girls to play raindrop butterflies and rainbow butterflies, and one girl to dance as the sunshine butterfly!"

Back home, Isabella told Mum all about the ballet show.

"I just wish I could remember my left from my right!" she sighed.

Mum smiled. "This might help." She gave Isabella a beautiful butterfly bracelet. "Wear it on your right wrist. Then you'll always be able to tell which way is right."

At each ballet lesson, Isabella kept looking at her butterfly bracelet to make sure she turned the right way!

Finally, after many rehearsals, Madame Colette gave the girls their roles.

"Isabella, you will play the sunshine butterfly. Because you twirl so beautifully, you will dance the final pirouette!" said Madame Colette.

Isabella smiled. She just hoped she would turn the right way!

The week before the show, Isabella practised her pirouettes everywhere! She twirled in the garden…in her bedroom…and at the park.

On the night of the big show, all the girls dressed in tutus and shimmering butterfly wings. The lights dimmed. Beautiful music filled the room. The ballet was about to begin!

The raindrop and rainbow butterflies danced gracefully from flower to flower.

At last, it was Isabella's turn to dance. Nervously, she touched her butterfly bracelet. Then, taking a deep breath, she twirled the most perfect pirouette she had ever twirled!

The girls joined Isabella on stage and they all curtsied.

"Oops!" giggled Isabella. She had curtsied with the wrong foot forward, but it didn't matter one little bit.

She would always be Isabella, Butterfly Ballerina!

The Old Woman and the Fat Hen

There was once an old woman who kept a hen that laid one egg every morning without fail. The eggs were large and delicious, and the old woman was able to sell them for a very good price at market.

"If my hen would lay two eggs every day," she said to herself, "I would be able to earn twice as much money!"

So, every evening, the old woman fed the hen twice as much food.

Each day, the old woman went to the henhouse expecting to find two eggs, but there was still only one – and the hen was getting fatter and fatter.

One morning, the woman looked in the nest box and there were no eggs at all. There were none the next day, nor any the day after that. All the extra food had made the hen so fat and contented that she had become lazy and had given up laying eggs altogether!

And the moral of the story is: things don't always work out as planned.

The Mice in Council

Once there was a large family of mice who lived in a big old house. Everything would have been perfect, except for one thing – the cat who lived there too. Each time the mice crept into the kitchen to nibble a few crumbs, the cat would pounce and chase them under the floorboards.

"If we don't come up with a plan soon, we'll starve!" cried Grandfather Mouse.

But the mice couldn't agree on a single idea. Finally, the youngest mouse had a brainwave.

"We could put a bell on the cat's collar, so we can hear him coming," he suggested.

All the mice thought this was an excellent plan.

Then, Grandfather Mouse stood up. "You are a very smart young fellow to come up with such an idea," he said, "but tell me – who is going to be brave enough to put the bell on the cat's collar?"

And the moral of the story is: it is sometimes easy to think of a clever plan, but it can be much more difficult to carry it out.

Snow White

Once there was a queen who longed for a daughter. As she sat sewing by her window one winter's day, she pricked her finger on the needle. As blood fell from her finger, she thought, "I wish I had a daughter with lips as red as blood, hair as black as ebony wood and skin as white as the snow outside!"

Before long, the queen gave birth to a baby girl with blood-red lips, ebony hair and skin as white as snow. The queen called her daughter Snow White.

Sadly, the queen died and the king married again. His new wife was beautiful, but vain.

She had a magic mirror, and every day she looked into it and asked:

"Mirror, mirror, on the wall,
Who is the fairest of them all?"

Every day, the mirror replied:

"You, O Queen, are the fairest of them all."

But Snow White became more and more beautiful every day. One morning, when the queen asked the mirror who was the fairest, the mirror replied:

"You, O Queen, are fair, it's true.
But young Snow White is fairer than you."

Furious, the queen told her huntsman, "Take Snow White into the forest and kill her!"

The huntsman led Snow White deep into the forest, but could not bear to hurt her. "Run far away from here," he said.

As darkness fell, Snow White came upon a little cottage. She knocked softly on the door, but there was no answer, so she let herself in. Inside, Snow White found a table and seven tiny chairs.

Upstairs, there were seven little beds.

Snow White lay down on the seventh bed and fell fast asleep.

She awoke to find seven little men staring at her in amazement.

"Who are you?" she asked.

"We are the seven dwarves who live here," said one dwarf. "Who are you?"

"I am Snow White," she replied, and she told them her sad story.

"You can stay with us," said the eldest dwarf, kindly.

Every day, the seven dwarves went to work while Snow White cooked and cleaned the cottage.

"Don't open the door to anyone," they told her, worried the wicked queen might find her.

Meanwhile, when the wicked queen asked her mirror once more who was the fairest that day, it replied:

"You, O Queen, are fair, it's true,
But Snow White is still fairer than you.
Deep in the forest with seven little men
Snow White is living in a cosy den."

The queen was furious and vowed to kill Snow White herself. So she added poison to a juicy apple and set off to the forest, disguised as a pedlar woman.

"Try my juicy apples!" she called out, knocking on the door of the seven dwarves' cottage.

Snow White remembered the dwarves' warning, so she opened only the window to take a look.

When the queen offered Snow White an apple, she took a big bite. The poisoned piece got stuck in her throat and she fell to the ground.

When the seven dwarves returned, they were heartbroken to find their beloved Snow White dead. They couldn't bear to bury her, so they put her in a glass coffin and placed it in the forest, where they took turns watching over her.

One day, a prince rode by and saw Snow White. The dwarves told him her sad story.

"Please let me take her away," begged the prince. The dwarves could see he loved Snow White and they agreed to let her go.

As the prince's servants lifted the coffin, one of them stumbled, jolting the poisoned apple from Snow White's throat, and she came back to life.

When Snow White saw the handsome prince, she fell deeply in love with him.

They soon married and lived happily ever after, together with the dwarves.

The Little Red Hen

There was once a little red hen who lived on a farm with her friends: a sleepy cat, a lazy pig and a stuck-up duck.

One day, the little red hen found some grains of wheat.

"If I plant these," she thought, "they will grow tall and strong, and make more wheat!"

She went to see her friends.

"Who will help me plant these grains of wheat?" she asked.

"Not I," mewed the cat.

"Not I," snorted the pig.

"Not I," quacked the duck.

So the little red hen planted the grains of wheat and tended to the growing wheat all summer. At last, the wheat was ready to harvest.

"Who will help me harvest the wheat?" the little red hen asked her friends.

"Not I," mewed the cat.

"Not I," snorted the pig.

"Not I," quacked the duck.

So the little red hen harvested the wheat, then went back to her friends.

"Who will help me carry the harvested wheat to the mill?" she asked.

"Not I," mewed the cat.

"Not I," snorted the pig.

"Not I," quacked the duck.

So the little red hen carried the heavy sack of wheat to the mill, where the kind miller ground it to flour.

"Who will help me bake a loaf of bread with this flour?" she asked.

"Not I," mewed the cat.

"Not I," snorted the pig.

"Not I," quacked the duck.

So the little red hen baked a loaf of bread all by herself.

"Who will help me eat this delicious bread?" the little red hen asked quietly.

"I will!" mewed the cat.

"I will!" snorted the pig.

"I will!" quacked the duck.

"No, you will not!" cried the little red hen. "I did all the work and no one helped. My chicks and I will eat the loaf!"

And the little red hen and her little chicks ate up every crumb of the hot, fresh bread.

Silly Billy

Bats do a lot of things upside down. They eat upside down. They sleep upside down. But Billy Bat spent so much time upside down that he thought up WAS down!

One night, Billy saw the reflection of the moon in the lake as he hung from his perch.

"I want to fly to the moon," he said.

"Don't be silly, Billy," said his sister, Grace. "The moon is too far away."

"No, it's not," said Billy, pointing to the reflection. "It's really close – look!"

Grace shook her head. "You don't understand!" she said.

But Billy wasn't listening.

"Here I go!" he cried. "Wheeee!" He spread his wings and zoomed towards the reflection of the moon in the water. SPLASH! Billy dived into the lake. A few seconds later, he crawled out, spluttering, and found his sister waiting for him.

"Do you understand now, Billy?" Grace asked.

"Yes," said Billy, shivering. "The moon is much, much wetter than it looks!"

What a silly Billy!

Fluff's Muddle

Fluff was all in a muddle. During the daytime, when owls should be asleep, Fluff was wide awake. There was just so much happening on the farm! She giggled at the geese waddling around the pond, and chuckled as the chickens scratched and pecked the ground. She laughed so much that she kept waking her family up.

"You're too noisy!" said her sister, Blink.

"You're keeping us awake!" said her brother, Beak.

That night, Fluff was feeling tired, just when owls should be wide awake.

"I know what we can do to fix Fluff's muddle," said Blink.

Fluff could hardly believe her eyes as Blink and Beak waddled round the pond like geese, and scratched and pecked the ground like chickens. She laughed so much that it kept her awake all night.

By the time morning came, Fluff was feeling very tired indeed. The geese waddled and the chickens scratched and pecked as usual, but Fluff was fast asleep.

The Princess and the Pea

Once upon a time, there lived a handsome prince. He had loving parents and plenty of friends, and lived a wonderful life in his castle. But one thing made him sad. He did not have a wife.

The prince had always wanted to marry a princess. But he wanted her to be clever and funny, and loving and kind. Not one of the princesses that he met at parties and balls was quite right.

Some of the princesses were too mean; some were too rude.

Some were too quiet; some were too loud.

And some were just plain boring!

So the prince decided to travel the world in the hope of finding a perfect princess. He met many more princesses who tried to impress him with their beauty, their dancing and their baking…but still none was quite right.

"I'm never going to meet the girl of my dreams," he sighed to himself.

"Cheer up, son," said the king. "You are still young. One day, you will meet a wonderful girl, just like I met your mother."

Several months later, when even the king and queen had begun to give up hope of their son ever finding a bride, there was a terrible storm. Suddenly, there was a loud knock on the castle door.

"I wonder who could be out on such a terrible stormy night?" said the prince. When he opened the door, a pretty young girl stared back at him. She was soaked from head to toe.

"Please may I come in for a moment?" she pleaded. "I was travelling to see some friends, but I got lost in this storm, and now I am very cold and wet."

"You poor thing," said the queen. "You must stay the night. You cannot travel on in this weather."

The prince smiled at the girl. "What is your name?"

"I'm Princess Penelope," she replied. "You are all very kind.
I don't want to be a bother to you."

At the word 'princess', the queen smiled to herself. She took the
girl's hand and said, "Of course not. Let's get you warm and dry."

Later, the prince listened contentedly as the charming princess
chatted away over supper. She was clever and funny, and loving
and kind. By the end of the evening, he'd fallen in love!

The queen was delighted when she saw what was happening,
but she wanted to be quite sure that Penelope was a real princess.

She went to the guest room in
the castle and placed a tiny
pea under the mattress.
Then, she told the
servants to pile twenty
more mattresses onto
the bed and twenty
feather quilts on top
of the twenty
mattresses!

The queen showed the princess to her room. "Sleep well, my dear," she said.

In the morning, the queen asked Penelope how she'd slept.

Penelope didn't want to be rude, but she couldn't lie. "I'm afraid I hardly slept a wink!" she replied.

"I'm so sorry," replied the queen. "Was the bed not comfortable?"

"There were so many lovely mattresses and quilts, it should have been very comfortable," replied the princess, "but I could feel something lumpy, and now I am black and blue all over!"

The queen grinned and hugged the girl to her. "That proves it!" she cried. "Only a real princess would be able to feel a tiny pea through twenty mattresses and twenty feather quilts!"

The prince was filled with joy. He had finally met the princess of his dreams!

Not long after that, the prince asked Princess Penelope to be his wife. They married and the prince was never unhappy again. And as for the pea? It was put in the royal museum as proof that perfect princesses do exist!

Chicken Licken

One day, an acorn fell on Chicken Licken's head, then rolled away.

"Oh, my!" clucked Chicken Licken, panicking. "THE SKY IS FALLING!"

"Cluck-a-cluck-cluck!" shrieked Henny Penny. "We must tell the king!"

So they flapped down the road and met Cocky Locky.

"Where are you going in such a hurry?" he asked.

"THE SKY IS FALLING!" cried Chicken Licken. "We're off to tell the king!"

"Cock-a-doodle-doo!" crowed Cocky Locky. "I'll come, too!"

So Chicken Licken, Henny Penny and Cocky Locky rushed off to tell the king. Soon, they met Ducky Lucky.

"Why are you flapping so?" she asked.

"THE SKY IS FALLING!" cried Chicken Licken. "We're off to tell the king!"

"C-can I c-c-come?" quacked Ducky Lucky nervously.

So Chicken Licken, Henny Penny, Cocky Locky and Ducky Lucky rushed off to tell the king.

Soon, they met Drakey Lakey.

"What's all this fuss?" he asked.

"THE SKY IS FALLING!" cried Chicken Licken. "We're off to tell the king!"

"I'll join you," squawked Drakey Lakey.

So Chicken Licken, Henny Penny, Cocky Locky, Ducky Lucky and Drakey Lakey rushed off to tell the king.

Soon, they met Goosey Loosey and Turkey Lurkey.

"What's ruffled your feathers?" Goosey Loosey asked.

"THE SKY IS FALLING!" cried Chicken Licken. "We're off to tell the king!"

"Goodness!" gobbled Turkey Lurkey.

"We'll come!" honked Goosey Loosey.

So Chicken Licken, Henny Penny, Cocky Locky, Ducky Lucky, Drakey Lakey, Goosey Loosey and Turkey Lurkey rushed off to tell the king.

Soon, they met Foxy Loxy.

"Hello!" he said. "Where are you all going?"

"THE SKY IS FALLING!" cried Chicken Licken. "We're off to tell the king!"

Foxy Loxy grinned slyly. "I know a short cut. Follow me."

So they did…right into Foxy Loxy's den!

"RUN!" cried Chicken Licken.

And the seven birds ran home, flapping and flurrying, as fast as they could.

And they never did get to tell the king about the sky falling.

Jungle Ballet

Milly Monkey didn't like the dark. She snuggled up on Granny Monkey's knee and tried not to look at it, but it was all around her.

"The dark isn't scary," said Granny Monkey. "Don't you know what happens at night when the stars come out?"

Milly shook her head.

"Sometimes, the jungle puts on a magical ballet," whispered Granny Monkey. "Little lights twirl and dance, but you can only see them if you're in bed."

Milly longed to see the ballet. Bravely, she climbed into bed and said goodnight. Then, Granny Monkey began to sing a beautiful lullaby. Her song called all the fireflies in the jungle and they danced around Milly's head until she fell asleep.

Next day, Milly told Granny Monkey, "You were right. Dark isn't scary. Dark is magical."

And Granny Monkey gave a wise old smile!

Brave Amy

Amy the ostrich wasn't like her ostrich friends. They were afraid of everything – from loud noises to sandstorms. And whenever anything scared them, they buried their heads in the sand. But Amy never did.

Amy dreamed of having adventures, but her friends just laughed. "Ostriches don't go travelling," they said. "It's much too scary."

One evening, the ostriches heard a big noise drifting across the plain. BANG! BANG! TOOT! TOOT! Of course, they all buried their heads in the sand. But not Amy – she stood up straight.

"I'm not scared," she said bravely.

In the evening light, she saw a travelling band marching towards her. They were playing drums and trumpets. BANG! BANG! TOOT! TOOT! And they all looked very happy.

"I like your band," Amy said shyly.

"Then join us!" said a camel with a drum.

Amy looked at her friends with their heads buried in the sand and she knew what she wanted to do.

Now, Amy has great adventures with the marching band and she bangs the loudest drum of all!

The Ugly Duckling

Once there was a proud and happy duck. "I have seven beautiful eggs and soon I will have seven beautiful ducklings," she told her friends on the riverbank.

A while later, she heard a CRACK! One beautiful duckling popped her little head out of a shell. And then another…and another…until there were six beautiful little ducklings, drying their fluffy yellow wings in the spring air.

"Just one egg left," quacked Mother Duck, "and it's a big one!"

For a while, nothing happened. Then, at last, the big egg began to hatch.

Tap, tap, tap! Out came a beak.

Crack, crack, crack! Out popped a head.

Crunch, crunch, crunch! Out came the last duckling.

"Oh, my!" gasped Mother Duck, "Isn't he…different?"

The last little duckling did look strange. He was bigger than the other ducklings and he didn't have such lovely yellow feathers.

"That's okay," said Mother Duck. "You may look different, but you're special to me."

When Mother Duck took her little ducklings for a swim, each one landed in the river with a little plop. But the ugly duckling fell over his big feet and landed in the water with a big SPLASH! The other ducklings laughed at their clumsy brother.

"Hush now, little chicks," said Mother Duck. "Stick together and stay behind me!"

Back at the nest, the ducklings practised their quacking.

"Quack, quack, quackety-quack!" said the ducklings, repeating after Mother Duck.

"Honk! Honk!" called the ugly duckling.

The other ducklings all quacked with laughter.

The ugly duckling hung his head in shame.

"I'll never fit in," he thought sadly.

The next day, Mother Duck took her little ones out for another swim. The little ducklings stayed close to her, while the ugly duckling swam alone.

"What kind of a bird are you?" asked some geese, who had landed on the river nearby.

"I'm a duckling," he replied. "My family has left me all alone."

The geese felt sorry for the ugly duckling and asked him to go with them. But the ugly duckling was too afraid to leave his river, so he stayed put.

When Mother Duck wasn't looking, the other ducklings teased their ugly brother.

"Look at his dull, grey feathers," said one of his sisters unkindly, admiring her own reflection in the water. "Mine are so much prettier."

The ugly duckling swam away and looked at his reflection.

"I don't look the same as them," he thought, sadly.

So he swam down the river and didn't stop until he'd reached a place he had never seen before. "I'll stay here," he decided.

Summer turned to autumn. The sky became cloudy and the river murky. But still the ugly duckling swam alone in his quiet part of the river.

Snow fell heavily that winter, and the ugly duckling was cold and lonely. The river was frozen solid.

"At least I can't see my ugly reflection any more," he thought.

Spring arrived at last and the ice thawed.

Some magnificent white ducks arrived on the river and swam towards the ugly duckling.

"You're very big ducks," he said, nervously.

"We're not ducks," laughed the elegant creatures. "We're swans – just like you!"

Puzzled, the ugly duckling looked at his reflection in the river, and was surprised to see beautiful white feathers and an elegant long neck.

"Is that really me?" he asked.

"Of course," they told him. "You are a truly handsome swan!"

The handsome young swan joined his new friends and glided gracefully back up the river with them.

When he swam past a family of ducks, Mother Duck recognized her ugly duckling straight away. "I always knew he was special," she said.

And the beautiful young swan swam down the river proudly, ruffling his spectacular white feathers and holding his elegant head high.

The Moonlight Tooth Fairy

Twinkle was a tooth fairy. Every night, she flew from house to house collecting the teeth that children had left under their pillows.

Each time she took a tooth, she slipped a shiny coin in its place. Twinkle loved to make people happy, but she often felt lonely. "I wish I had a friend," she thought.

One night, Twinkle came to Isla's house. As she flew through the open window, she felt somebody watching her. A fairy face stared at her in the moonlight. And another. There were fairy pictures and toys everywhere!

Twinkle was so surprised, she dropped the coin. The noise woke Isla.

Isla gasped when she spotted Twinkle.

Twinkle started to cry. "You've seen me! I've broken the most important fairy rule!"

"Don't cry!" said Isla, gazing at Twinkle in amazement. "I won't tell anyone, I promise."

"And I've lost your coin!" sobbed Twinkle.

Isla had an idea. "Instead of giving me a coin, could you grant me a fairy wish?" she asked.

"What would you wish for?" said Twinkle, drying her tears.

"I wish to be a fairy just like you!"

Twinkle waved magic into the room.

Suddenly, Isla felt herself shrinking.

"I'm growing wings!" she cried with joy. "Will you teach me how to fly?"

"It's easy!" said Twinkle. "Hold my hand…"

Twinkle led Isla out into the moonlit garden. They flew between the trees and skimmed a starry pond.

"I love being a fairy!" cried Isla.

"It's much more fun with two," laughed Twinkle happily. At last she had a real friend of her own.

Soon, it was time for Isla to go back to being a little girl. "Thank you for making my wish come true," she said to Twinkle.

"You've made my wish come true, too!" replied Twinkle.

Twinkle promised to come back soon.

As she flew away, she whispered, "Sweet dreams, my fairy friend!"

Jade's First Race

It was Jade the green car's first ever race. She was very excited and she couldn't stop grinning.

"I hope I get a medal!" she cried.

But, around the first bend in the track, she saw Ruby the red car, with a burst tyre. So Jade stopped to replace it.

Around the next bend, Yasmin the yellow car called for help.

"Need water!" she panted. So Jade gave her some water.

Around the next bend, she saw Ben the blue car.

"I've run out of petrol!" Ben spluttered.

Jade lent him some petrol and Ben zoomed off.

After helping all the other cars, Jade finished the race in last place.

"I'll never get a medal now," she sighed, dipping her headlights as the other cars gathered around.

"Jade came last because she stopped to help us," said Ruby.

"She's the real winner," said Yasmin.

"Jade deserves a medal," said Ben. "Three cheers for the kindest car in the race!"

Brown Bear's Bus Ride

Every day, a shiny blue bus full of people roared past Brown Bear's home.

"I wish I could ride on the bus," he murmured. "I wonder where it goes?"

Then, one morning, a bus ticket fluttered onto the grass outside his cave. He picked it up with trembling paws. His dream had come true!

When Brown Bear climbed onto the bus, the driver stalled the engine in shock and the passengers squealed. Brown Bear couldn't understand why everyone looked so scared. But one little girl wasn't afraid.

"Hello," she smiled, slipping her hand into his paw. "I'm Ella."

When the other passengers saw how brave Ella was, they felt silly. They all shook hands with Brown Bear as the bus set off past the farm, through the town and over the bridges. Now he knew where the bus went!

At the end of his ride, Ella kissed him and the passengers hugged him goodbye.

"Come back soon," they said. "This bus is now bear-friendly!"

Rapunzel

Once upon a time, a poor young couple lived in a cottage next door to an old witch. The witch grew many vegetables in her garden, but she kept them all for herself.

One day, the couple had only a few potatoes left to eat.

"Surely it wouldn't matter if we took just a few vegetables?" said the wife, gazing longingly over the wall.

So her husband quickly climbed into the garden and started to fill his basket. Suddenly, he heard an angry voice.

"How dare you steal my vegetables!"

"Please don't hurt me," begged the young man. "My wife is going to have a baby soon!"

"You may keep the vegetables," she croaked. "But you must give me the baby when it is born." Terrified, the man had to agree.

Months later, the woman gave birth to a little girl. And although the parents begged and cried, the cruel witch took the baby. She called her Rapunzel.

Years passed, and Rapunzel grew up to be kind and beautiful. The witch was so afraid of losing her that she built a tall tower with no door and only one window. She planted thorn bushes all around it, then locked Rapunzel in the tower.

Each day, Rapunzel brushed and combed her long, golden locks.

Each day, the witch came to visit her, standing at the foot of the tower and calling out, "Rapunzel, Rapunzel, let down your hair!"

Rapunzel hung her hair out of the window, and the witch climbed up it to sit and talk with her. But Rapunzel was very lonely. Each day, she sat at her window and sang sadly.

One day, a prince rode by and heard the beautiful singing coming from the witch's garden. As he hid behind the wall, he saw the old witch call out, "Rapunzel, Rapunzel, let down your hair!"

The prince saw a cascade of golden hair fall from the tower and he watched the witch climb up it.

When the witch returned to her house, he crept to the tower. "Rapunzel, Rapunzel, let down your hair," he called softly.

Rapunzel let down her locks and the prince climbed up.

Rapunzel was very surprised to see the prince and delighted when he said he wanted to be her friend. From then on, the prince came to visit her every day.

Months passed, and Rapunzel and the prince fell in love.

"How can we be together?" Rapunzel cried. "The witch will never let me go."

So the prince brought some silk, which Rapunzel knotted together to make a ladder, so that she could escape from the tower.

One day, without thinking, Rapunzel remarked to the witch, "It's much harder to pull you up than the prince!"

The witch was furious! "What prince?" she shouted.

She grabbed Rapunzel's long hair and cut it off. Then, she used her magic to send Rapunzel far into the forest.

That evening, when the prince came to see Rapunzel, the witch held the golden hair out of the window and he climbed up into the tower, coming face to face with the old witch.

"You will never see Rapunzel again!" she screamed, and pushed the prince out of the window. He fell into the thorn bushes below. The sharp spikes scratched his eyes and blinded him. Weeping, he stumbled away.

After months of wandering, blind and lost, the prince heard beautiful, sad singing floating through the woods. He recognized Rapunzel's voice and called out to her.

"At last I have found you!" she cried. As her tears fell onto the prince's eyes, his wounds healed, and he could see again.

Rapunzel had never been so happy. She and the prince were soon married, and they lived happily ever after, far away from the old witch and her empty tower.

The Three Little Pigs

Once upon a time, three little pigs lived together with their mother. One day, it was time for them to leave home and build houses of their own.

"Be careful of the big, bad wolf," warned their mother as they trotted off down the road.

The first little pig built his house from straw.

Before long, the big, bad wolf came to call.

"Little pig, little pig, let me come in," growled the wolf, licking his lips. He had come for his supper.

"Not by the hairs on my chinny-chin-chin!" the first little pig replied.

"Well, I'll huff and I'll puff and I'll blow your house down!" snarled the wolf. And that's just what he did. The little pig ran away as fast as he could.

The second little pig decided to build his house from sticks.

When the wolf saw the house, he pushed his nose against the door and growled, "Little pig, little pig, let me come in."

"Not by the hairs on my chinny-chin-chin!" cried the second little pig.

"Well, I'll huff and I'll puff and I'll blow your house down!" snarled the wolf. And that's just what he did. The little pig ran away as fast as he could.

The third little pig built a strong house from bricks. He had just put a pot of soup on the fire to boil when he saw his brothers running down the path, closely followed by the wolf.

"Quick!" cried the third little pig. He opened the door and let his brothers inside.

"Little pigs, little pigs, let me come in!" roared the wolf.

"Not by the hairs on our chinny-chin-chins!" cried the three little pigs.

"Well, I'll huff and I'll puff and I'll blow your house down!" snarled the wolf. So he huffed and he puffed…and he huffed and he puffed…but the house stood firm.

The wolf climbed onto the roof and slid down the chimney – straight into the pot of hot soup.

"Owwwoooo!" he cried.

The wolf leapt up and ran out of the house, never to be seen again!

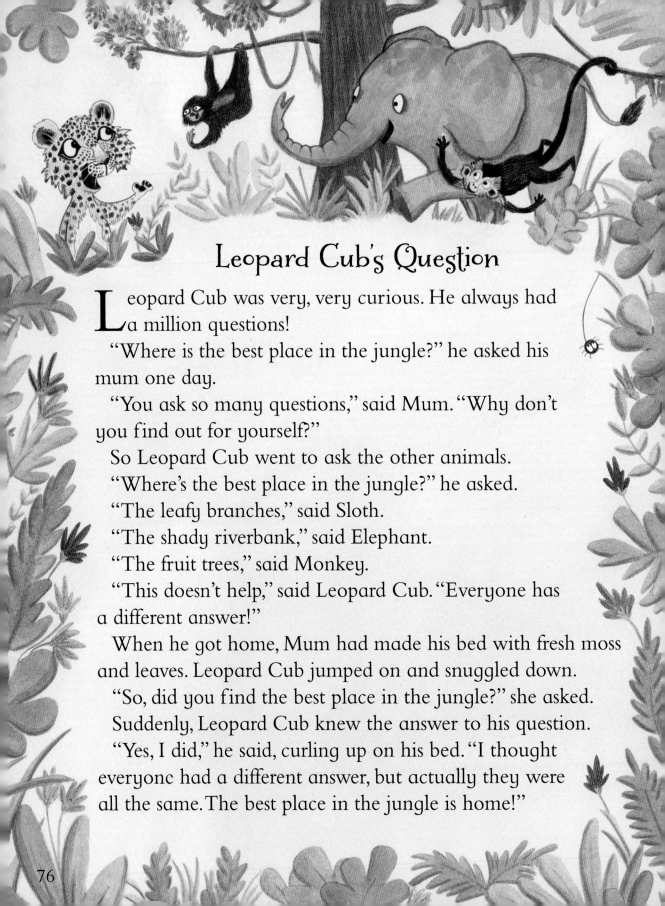

Leopard Cub's Question

Leopard Cub was very, very curious. He always had a million questions!

"Where is the best place in the jungle?" he asked his mum one day.

"You ask so many questions," said Mum. "Why don't you find out for yourself?"

So Leopard Cub went to ask the other animals.

"Where's the best place in the jungle?" he asked.

"The leafy branches," said Sloth.

"The shady riverbank," said Elephant.

"The fruit trees," said Monkey.

"This doesn't help," said Leopard Cub. "Everyone has a different answer!"

When he got home, Mum had made his bed with fresh moss and leaves. Leopard Cub jumped on and snuggled down.

"So, did you find the best place in the jungle?" she asked.

Suddenly, Leopard Cub knew the answer to his question.

"Yes, I did," he said, curling up on his bed. "I thought everyone had a different answer, but actually they were all the same. The best place in the jungle is home!"

Crocodiles Don't Wear Pyjamas

There was just one thing that Christopher Crocodile wanted – a pair of pyjamas.

"Crocodiles don't wear pyjamas," said his father. "We're too tough and scaly and scary."

But Christopher had seen a little boy wearing them once and he had never forgotten.

"Try making some yourself," suggested his mother.

So Christopher gathered large, colourful leaves and star-shaped flowers, and made the most magnificent pair of starry pyjamas.

"You look fantastic!" said his mother.

"Fabulous!" said his friends.

All the crocodiles in the swamp started asking for a pair of Christopher's pyjamas. He made more…and more…and more!

Nowadays, when the sun is shining, crocodiles look just as tough and scaly and scary as ever. But when the moon comes out and it's time for bed, every single one pulls on a wonderful pair of pyjamas.

Even Christopher's father!

Bunny Loves to Read

Buster Bunny loved books. He read stories of princes…and pirates…and witches and wizards. He read books about trains…and dinosaurs.

One day, Buster's friends came over.

"Hi, Buster!" they said. "Are you coming out to play?"

"Sure," said Buster with a smile, "when I've finished my book. It's all about pirates!"

"You've always got your nose in a book!" said his sister Bella. "Hopscotch is more fun!"

"Books are boring!" croaked Francine the frog. "Why read books when you can play leapfrog?"

"Racing each other is even more fun," said Max the mouse.

"Don't listen to them, Buster," said Sam the squirrel. "I think books are the best!"

"Really?" asked Buster.

"Yes," said Sam, smiling. "Books are the best – for nibbling!"

"Hey!" laughed Buster.

Then Bella said, "Come on, let's leave Buster with his dumb old books and play outside!"

But it was raining. The friends looked out of the window gloomily.

"Why don't you read some of my books?" asked Buster, bringing out a big box.

"We don't want to look at books," said Sam grumpily. "We're only waiting for the rain to stop."

Buster took a book out of the box.

"There's a big thunderstorm in this story," said Buster. "It's all about pirates hunting for buried treasure."

"Buried treasure?" asked Sam. "Like nuts and acorns? Yum!"

"Not exactly," replied Buster. "But it's very exciting. Take a look."

"I guess there's nothing better to do," sighed Sam.

"Frogs really hate being stuck inside!" grumbled Francine.

"This book is about a prince who turns into a frog," Buster said.

"Good for him," said Francine. "Does he turn back into a prince?"

"Why don't you read it and find out?" smiled Buster.

79

"Being cooped up inside is making me sleepy," said Max.

Buster gave Max a book. "The princess in this story goes to sleep for a hundred years!" he said.

"Really? Wow! How does she wake up?"

"Read it and see!" said Buster.

"Well, okay, but I might fall asleep before I finish it!"

"I'm bored! I'm going to get a cookie," said Bella. "Hey, Buster, your box is in my way!"

"Can't you just step over it?"

"Only if I take a giant step," said Bella.

"Just like a dinosaur!" said Buster. "Some of them were bigger than a house!"

Buster looked out the window. "Hey, it's stopped raining!" he cried. "Who's coming out to play?"

"Shh! I'm still reading. The pirates haven't found the treasure yet!" said Sam.

"And the prince is still a frog!" croaked Francine.

"And the brave knight is still searching for the sleeping princess!" cried Max.

"And I've just got to a good part about *Tyrannosaurus rex*!" laughed Bella.

"So what do you want to play outside?" asked Buster when the friends had all finished reading. "Hopscotch? Leapfrog? Tag?"

"Let's pretend we can do magic spells. If you give me a kiss, I'll turn into a princess!" said Francine.

"Ugh! No thanks!" laughed Sam. "Let's play pirates!"

"Look out," said Bella. "I'm a *Tyrannosaurus!* ROOAAR!"

"I'm off to find the enchanted princess!" cried Max.

They played pirates and dinosaurs, and princes and princesses, until it was time to go home.

"Do you have any other books about dinosaurs?" asked Bella.

"Sure!" said Buster.

"What about frogs?" asked Francine.

"Yes," said Buster. "And toads too."

"Anything else about witches and magic?" asked Max.

"Loads!"

"Can I borrow another pirate story?" Sam asked.

"Of course you can," laughed Buster, "as long as you promise not to eat it!"

I Love My Daddy

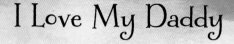

One day, Little Squirrel wanted to show Daddy Squirrel all the things he could do.

"What shall we do first?" said Daddy.

"Digging!" said Little Squirrel excitedly, as he dug and dug, with his little tail wagging.

"Well done!" said Daddy. But suddenly, Little Squirrel's tail stopped wagging.

"Help, Daddy! I'm stuck!"

Daddy Squirrel helped Little Squirrel wriggle out of the hole and gave him a hug.

"You are a good digger!" said Daddy. "What shall we play next?"

"Climbing!" said Little Squirrel, and he climbed as high as he could go.

"Well done!" said Daddy. But suddenly Little Squirrel closed his eyes tightly.

"Help, Daddy! I'm stuck!"

Daddy Squirrel helped Little Squirrel climb down and gave him a hug.

"You are a good climber!" said Daddy. "What shall we play next?"

"Jumping!" said Little Squirrel, and he jumped with a big smile on his face. But suddenly Little Squirrel stopped smiling and… SPLAT! He was in the mud.

"Help, Daddy! I'm stuck again!"

Daddy Squirrel helped Little Squirrel out of the sticky patch of mud and gave him a hug.

"You are good at jumping!" said Daddy.

But Little Squirrel shook his head sadly.

"I can't do anything!" cried Little Squirrel. "I always get stuck!"

Daddy Squirrel lifted Little Squirrel onto his shoulders.

"Let's play together," he said. "Let's run!"

Little Squirrel held on tightly as they whooshed through the woods.

"Yippee!" he shouted.

"Let's climb!" said Daddy Squirrel. Little Squirrel kept his eyes open wide as they reached the top of a tree.

"Wheeee!" he shouted.

"And now," said Daddy Squirrel, "let's jump!"

SPLAT!

"Oh, help!" cried Daddy Squirrel. "Now I'm stuck!"

Little Squirrel giggled as he helped his daddy out of the sticky mud.

"You can do everything, Little Squirrel!" said Daddy proudly. "You can even save a Daddy Squirrel!"

Little Squirrel grinned.

"I love playing with you… and I love my daddy!" he shouted, and they raced home happily together.

The Perfect Pet

Emily was visiting her friend Ethan's farm to choose a puppy. Most of the puppies bounded around the barn, barking and jumping on each other. But one puppy pressed gently against Emily's legs and licked her knees.

"I like this one," said Emily, looking at the puppy's cute brown fur.

"Are you sure?" asked Ethan. "Rusty doesn't chase sticks and run around like the other puppies."

Rusty's ears drooped and he pressed closer to Emily. It was true he wasn't like the others. But Emily looked down at his sad eyes and smiled at him.

"Look, he's so gentle and kind," said Emily, tickling Rusty's ears. "He's the perfect pet for me!"

Rusty's heart leapt with happiness and he wagged his little tail. And Emily knew that she had found the most perfect pet in the whole wide world.

The Secret Cat Circus

Every morning, when they went to work, Jessie's owners left her dozing in the sunniest corner of the garden. They thought she was a very sleepy cat, but Jessie had a secret. As soon as they had gone, Jessie pulled on a sparkly costume and went to work too…at the cat circus hidden at the bottom of their garden!

"Roll up!" the tabby circus master shouted to the gathering crowd. "Come and see the best tightrope-walking cat in the whole wide world!"

The crowd gasped as Jessie walked the tightrope, balancing a fish on her nose and juggling balls of string.

By five o'clock, the circus show was over and Jessie pulled off her costume, settling down to doze in the sun for when her owners came home.

"That cat could sleep all day!" Jessie's owners cried each evening.

Little did they know of her performing talent – or where the sparkles in her fur came from!

Alice and the White Rabbit

One day, Alice was sitting beside a river with her sister, when something curious happened – a white rabbit with pink eyes ran past.

"Oh, dear! Oh, dear! I shall be too late!" he said. Then, he took a watch out of his vest pocket and hurried on.

Alice followed the rabbit down a large rabbit hole. The rabbit hole went straight on like a tunnel for some way and then dipped so suddenly that she found herself falling down…

"I must be getting near the centre of the Earth," Alice thought to herself. Down, down, down. Alice kept falling.

Suddenly, she landed in a heap at the bottom. When she got up, she found herself in a long hall, lined with doors. At the end was a little, three-legged, glass table. There was nothing on it but a tiny golden key. Alice tried the key in all the doors, but it wouldn't open any of them. Then, she noticed a low curtain she had not seen before. Behind it was a tiny door.

She turned the key in the lock and it opened. The door led into a beautiful garden, but Alice could not even get her head through the doorway. She went back to the table and saw a little bottle labelled "DRINK ME!"

Once she was sure it wasn't poison, Alice drank it and shrank. But she remembered that she had left the key on the table. Alice didn't know what to do. Then, she saw a cake marked "EAT ME!"

Alice ate it and began to grow. Soon, she was so large that her head touched the ceiling!

Alice began to cry. She was wondering what to do when who should come along but the white rabbit. He was carrying a pair of white gloves and a large fan.

"If you please, sir…" began Alice.

The rabbit dropped the gloves and fan, and scurried away.

"How strange everything is today," said Alice, picking up the gloves and the fan. "I'm not myself at all." Then she began fanning herself as she wondered who she might be instead.

After a while, Alice looked down at her hands. She was surprised to see that she had put on one of the rabbit's little white gloves.

"I must be growing smaller again," she thought.

Alice realized that it was the fan that was making her shrink, so she dropped it quickly and ran to the door. Suddenly, she remembered that the key was still on the table.

"Drat," she said. "Things can't possibly get any worse." But she was wrong. SPLASH! She fell into her sea of tears.

"I wish I hadn't cried so much!" wailed Alice.

Just then, she heard something splashing. It was a mouse.

"Mouse, do you know the way out of this pool?" asked Alice.

The mouse didn't reply.

"Perhaps he speaks French," thought Alice. So she began again.

"*Où est mon chat?*" which was the first sentence in her French book and meant "Where is my cat?"

The mouse leapt out of the water in fright.

"I'm sorry!" cried Alice. "I didn't mean to scare you."

"Come ashore," said the mouse. "I'll tell you why cats frighten me."

By this time, the pool was crowded with birds and animals. There was a duck, a dodo, a parrot, an eaglet and other curious creatures, too. Together, they all swam to the shore.

The birds and animals were dripping wet.

"Let's have a race," said the dodo. "It will help us to dry off." And he began to mark out a course.

Then, when everyone was dotted along the course, they began starting and stopping whenever they felt like it. It was impossible to tell when the race was over, but after half an hour they were all very dry.

"But who won the race?" asked the mouse.

"Everyone," said the dodo. "Alice will give out prizes." So Alice handed around some sweets she had in her pocket.

"But she must have a prize, too," said the mouse.

"What else do you have in your pocket?" asked the dodo.

Alice handed over a thimble and he gave it back to her, saying, "I beg you to accept this thimble."

Alice accepted as solemnly as she could and then they all sat down to hear the mouse's tale. But Alice was so tired, she just couldn't concentrate, and she drifted off to sleep.

The next moment, she woke to the sound of her sister's voice. "Wake up, Alice!" said her sister. "What a long sleep you've had!"

"I've had such a curious dream!" said Alice, who told her sister all about it. And what a wonderful dream it had been.

A Drink for Blaze the Dragon

It was a very hot day and Blaze's mother was sleeping in the cool cave. But Blaze didn't want to sleep. He wanted to whizz around the mountain. He crept outside.

Wheeee! But flying around in the sizzling heat soon made Blaze thirsty. He flopped down by the lake at the bottom of the valley. Then, he remembered his mother's warning.

"Dragons can ONLY drink juniper juice!" she'd told him.

Blaze watched eagerly as a flock of birds drank from the lake. He was too hot to fly all the way home for juniper juice. Surely a little water wouldn't hurt? He licked up a few drops.

"Delicious," Blaze gasped. He dipped his whole face into the lake and the cold water rushed into his mouth.

Suddenly…PFFFT! Blaze's dragon flames went out.

Blaze was terrified. He flew home as fast as he could.

"Mum," he cried. "I'm not a dragon any more. Look! My fire has gone out!"

"Did you drink the lake water?" asked his mother sternly.

"I did!" he sobbed. "I didn't listen to you."

"There's only one way to get your fire back," she sighed. "We'll have to fly to the volcano. You must swallow its heat."

The burning volcano rumbled and crackled with molten lava as Blaze and his mother flew towards it.

Shaking with fear, the young dragon swooped down as low as he dared and took in a deep, fiery breath.

Blaze landed in the valley below, coughing and spluttering. Suddenly, flickers of orange fire shot out of his nose.

"Mum, it worked – I've got my fire back!" he cried.

Blaze's mother couldn't stay cross with him any more.

"Let's go home," she laughed. "Breathing in that volcano fire must have made you thirsty…for a nice glass of juniper juice!"

Not-So-Scary

Glob the monster longed to be big and scary, but he had never frightened anyone. He had never even made anyone jump.

"I'm just too nice," he thought to himself. "Monsters aren't supposed to be friendly!"

One day, at monster school, Glob saw a purple monster with yellow spots, called Murkle. Glob jumped out from behind a wall to try to scare her. ROAR!

He was pleased to see she was crying.

"Are you crying because I scared you?" asked Glob.

Murkle shook her head.

"I'm crying because I've got no one to share my sweets with," she said.

"Oh," said Glob, disappointed. "I've never tried sweets before."

Murkle held out the bag with a big monster smile.

"Try one," she said.

Together, Glob and Murkle munched up the whole bag. By the time they had finished the last one, they were best friends. They both decided never to scare anyone again.

"Sweets are delicious!" said Glob. "And I think being friendly is better than being scary."

Monster Nursery

Monster nursery is a lot like normal nursery. There are teachers and toys and books. But, of course, not everything is the same.

At monster nursery, you have to be NOISY! The teachers tell you off for walking because you're supposed to run everywhere. If you make a big mess when you eat, then you'd fit right in at monster nursery.

Every morning, the little monsters sing a special song.

"Naughty monsters just like me
Love to shout and sing!
Let's all make a dreadful mess
And jump on everything!"

Then they practise making rude noises and bouncing on cushions.

In the afternoon, the little monsters do painting, just like you. But they don't paint on paper. They paint on each other!

I'm afraid only little monsters are allowed to go to monster nursery, so you will just have to read about it here instead. Unless, of course, you're a little monster too!

Sleeping Beauty

Once upon a time, a king and queen had a beautiful baby girl. The proud parents decided to hold a christening feast to celebrate, so they invited kings, queens, princes and princesses from other kingdoms.

Five good fairies lived in the kingdom and the king wanted them to be godmothers to his daughter. One of these fairies was very old and no one had seen her in years, or even knew where she was. So, when the king sent out the invitations, he invited only the four young fairies.

The day of the christening arrived, and the palace was full of laughter and dancing.

After the delicious feast, the four fairies gave the princess their magical gifts.

The first fairy waved her wand over the crib and said, "You shall be kind and considerate."

The second fairy said, "You shall be beautiful and loving."

The third fairy said, "You shall be clever and thoughtful."

Suddenly, the palace doors flew open. It was the old fairy. She was furious because she hadn't been invited to the feast.

She flew up to the crib and waved her wand over the princess.

"One day, the king's daughter shall prick her finger on a spindle and fall down dead!" she screeched, and then rushed out.

"I cannot undo the spell," said the fourth fairy, "but I can soften it. The princess will prick her finger on a spindle, but she will not die. Instead, the princess, and everyone within the palace and its grounds, will fall into a deep sleep for a hundred years."

The king thanked the fairy and then, to protect his daughter, ordered every spindle in the kingdom to be burned.

The years passed, and the princess grew into a beautiful, clever and kind young woman.

One day, the princess decided to explore some rooms in the palace that she had never visited before. After a while, she came to a little door at the top of a tall tower. Inside, there was an old woman working at her spinning wheel. The princess didn't know that the woman was really the old fairy in disguise.

"What are you doing?" the princess asked curiously.

"I'm spinning thread, dear," replied the woman.

"Can I try?" asked the princess.

No sooner had she touched the spindle than she pricked her finger and fell into a deep sleep.

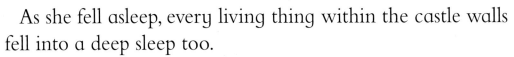

As she fell asleep, every living thing within the castle walls fell into a deep sleep too.

As time passed, a hedge of thorns sprang up around the palace. It grew higher and thicker every year, until only the tallest towers could be seen above it.

The story of the beautiful princess who lay sleeping within its walls spread throughout the land. She became known as Sleeping Beauty. Many princes tried to break through the thorns to rescue Sleeping Beauty, but none were successful.

Exactly 100 years after the princess had fallen asleep, a handsome prince, having heard the story of Sleeping Beauty, decided to try to awaken the sleeping princess.

The prince didn't know that the fairy's spell was coming to its end. As he pushed against the thick hedge, every thorn turned into a beautiful rose and a magic path formed to let him pass.

Soon, the prince came to the palace. He saw people and animals asleep in every room.

At last, he found the tiny room in the tower where Sleeping Beauty lay. He kissed her gently.

The sleeping princess opened her eyes and smiled. With that one look, they fell in love.

All around the palace, people started waking up. The spell had been broken!

The king called for a huge wedding feast to be prepared and this time he invited every person, and fairy, in the entire kingdom.

Sleeping Beauty married her handsome prince and they lived happily ever after.

The Three Billy Goats Gruff

Long ago, there were three brothers – a little goat, a medium-sized goat and a big goat.

The brothers lived in a field of short, dry grass beside a river.

On the other side of the river, over a bridge, was a huge meadow with long, juicy grass.

The goats longed to taste the juicy grass, but the bridge was guarded by a horrible, ugly troll.

One day, the little Billy Goat Gruff plucked up his courage and trotted over the bridge.

TRIP TRAP, TRIP TRAP went his feet.

"Who's that TRIP-TRAPPING over my bridge?" cried the troll, leaping in front of the little goat. "I will eat you!"

"Please don't!" cried the little goat. "Wait for my brother – he is much bigger and tastier than me."

"All right," said the greedy troll, and he let the little goat cross.

Later that day, the medium-sized goat saw his little brother munching juicy grass on the other side and wanted to eat it, too.

So he set off, TRIP TRAP, TRIP TRAP, across the bridge.

"Who's that TRIP-TRAPPING over my bridge?" cried the troll again. "I will eat you!"

"Please don't!" cried the medium-sized goat. "Wait for my brother — he is much bigger and tastier than me."

The greedy troll licked his lips and let the medium-sized Billy Goat Gruff cross the bridge.

At last, it was the big Billy Goat Gruff's turn to cross the bridge. TRIP TRAP, TRIP TRAP went his hooves on the wooden bridge.

"Who's that TRIP-TRAPPING over my bridge?" bellowed the troll, drooling at the sight of the big goat. "I will eat you!"

But the big Billy Goat Gruff was not afraid of the ugly troll.

"You can't eat me!" shouted the big Billy Goat Gruff.

He lowered his head, stamped his hooves and tossed the troll into the river with his great big billy goat horns.

Then, the biggest goat went TRIP TRAP, TRIP TRAP over the bridge to join his brothers, and the horrible troll never bothered them again!

Counting Stars

Tomorrow was to be Little Panda's first day at school and she was very excited. Daddy tucked her up in bed, but she was too wide awake to close her eyes.

"I wonder what new friends I'll meet," she said. "I can't wait to find my desk and meet my teacher. School is going to be so much fun!"

Daddy tried to make Little Panda feel sleepy. He read stories, he sang lullabies and he stroked her soft fur, but she was still wide awake.

"All right," he said. "Whatever you do, don't go to sleep. You must stay awake until you have counted every single star in the sky."

The sky was crowded with twinkling stars. Little Panda started to count them.

"One…two…three…four…"

Before she even reached number ten, Little Panda's eyelids had drooped and she'd fallen fast asleep.

And what did she dream about? Her first day at school, of course!

Lion's First Day

It was clumsy Lion's first day at Miss Giraffe's Savannah School. True to his nature, he arrived late, skidded into the classroom, tripped over his paws and landed upside down in his chair.

Miss Giraffe tilted her head and smiled kindly at Lion.

"What an amazing acrobat you are!" she said.

At lunchtime, Lion bumped into the table and knocked all the food over. Then he spilled his drink and slipped across the floor.

"What wonderful clown skills you have!" said Miss Giraffe.

At playtime, Lion tripped over and knocked some balls off a shelf, catching three with his paws and one on the tip of his tail.

"What a fantastic juggler you'd make!" said Miss Giraffe.

That evening, Lion couldn't wait to tell his mother about his day.

"All this time I thought I was clumsy, but Miss Giraffe thinks I'm an acrobat!" he said. "And a clown and a juggler!"

His mother smiled.

"You can be a magician too – just make your dinner disappear!"

Hansel and Gretel

Once upon a time, there were two children called Hansel and Gretel. They lived in a small cottage at the edge of the forest with their father, a poor woodcutter, and their stepmother.

One evening, the family had nothing left to eat but a few crusts of bread. Hansel and Gretel went to bed hungry. As they lay in their beds, they heard their parents talking.

"There are too many mouths to feed," said their stepmother. "We must take the children into the thickest part of the forest and leave them there."

"Never!" cried their father.

But the next morning, Hansel and Gretel's stepmother woke them early.

"Get up!" she ordered. "We're going into the forest to chop wood."

She handed them each a crust of bread for their lunch.

With a heavy heart, the woodcutter led his children into the forest. As they walked along, Hansel secretly dropped a trail of breadcrumbs along the path.

When they reached the middle of the forest, the woodcutter said, "Wait here. We'll return at sunset."

Hansel and Gretel waited all day, but their father and stepmother didn't come back. Soon, it was dark among the thick trees and Gretel was frightened.

"Don't worry," said Hansel, cuddling his sister. "We'll follow the trail of breadcrumbs I dropped along the path. It will lead us home."

But when the moon came up, they couldn't see any crumbs.

"Oh, no! The birds must have eaten them all!" whispered Hansel.

Hansel and Gretel curled up under a tree and fell fast asleep.

The next morning, they wandered through the forest until they came to a little cottage made of gingerbread and sweets!

The children were so hungry that they picked sweets off the house and crammed them into their mouths.

Just then, the door opened and an old woman hobbled out.

"Come in, children," she said, smiling. "I've got plenty more food in here."

The old woman fed them well and then put them to bed. But Hansel and Gretel didn't know that the old woman was actually a wicked witch who liked to eat children!

When Hansel and Gretel woke up, the witch grabbed Hansel and locked him in a cage. She set Gretel to work cooking huge meals to fatten up Hansel.

The weeks went by and every morning the witch went up to the cage, asking Hansel to hold out his finger.

"I want to feel if you are fat enough to eat," she said.

Hansel, being a smart boy, held out an old chicken bone instead. The witch's eyesight was so bad that she thought the bone was Hansel's finger.

One day, the witch got tired of waiting for the boy to get fatter and decided to cook him right away.

Grabbing Gretel's arm, she said, "Go and check if the oven is hot enough." And she pushed Gretel towards the open oven door. Grinning horribly, she licked her cracked lips. She was planning to eat Gretel too and couldn't wait for her delicious meal.

"I'm too big to fit in there," said Gretel, guessing the witch's wicked plan.

"You silly girl," cackled the witch. "Even I could fit in there." And she stuck her head inside. With a great big shove, Gretel pushed the witch into the oven and slammed the door shut.

"Hansel, the witch is dead!" cried Gretel, unlocking her brother's cage.

As the children made their way out of the house, they found chests crammed with gold and sparkling jewels. They filled their pockets and set off home.

Their father was overjoyed to see them. He told them that their stepmother had died while they were gone, so they had nothing to fear any more. Hansel and Gretel showed their father the treasure.

"We will never go hungry again!" he cried.

And they all lived happily ever after.

Surprise at the Shops

When Benjamin Mouse saw a blue bike in the toyshop window, Mr Mouse said bikes were silly. Benjamin thought his daddy was a bit too serious.

"Help me do the shopping instead," Mr Mouse said.

"Shopping is boring," grumbled Benjamin.

"Perhaps it'll be more fun than you think," said Mr Mouse.

At the grocer's, Mr Mouse picked out some carrots and some apples. Out of the corner of his eye, Benjamin saw the grocer juggle some apples and oranges. He told his daddy, who frowned.

"Grocers are too sensible to juggle," he said.

At the dairy, while Mr Mouse collected some milk and cheese, Benjamin saw Mrs Cow twirling in a pink tutu. He told his daddy, who shook his head.

"Cows are far too busy to dance," he said.

The final stop was the bakery. While Mr Mouse was busy choosing some rolls and buns for tea, Benjamin saw the baker balancing fifteen doughnuts on the tip of her nose. Benjamin told his daddy, who sighed.

"You're imagining things," he said. "Bakers don't play with their food."

As they passed the toyshop on the way home, the door opened and the toymaker wheeled out the blue bike.

"Oh, no," gasped Benjamin. "It's been sold!"

"Yes, it has," said the toymaker. "It belongs to YOU!"

Benjamin stared at his daddy in amazement.

"Did you buy it?" he asked.

"Me?" Mr Mouse said. "I'm far too serious to buy toys!"

But he exchanged a secret wink with the toymaker as Benjamin jumped onto the bike in excitement.

"I'll help with the shopping again tomorrow," Benjamin promised. "You were right – it's much more fun than I thought!"

Little Tiger Makes a Splash

Little Tiger hated water. He never took a bath and he refused to swim in the cool pool, even on the hottest of days.

"You're filthy and your fur is smelly! You need a wash," said Mummy Tiger one day.

"I like being muddy and tangled," Little Tiger replied, and sloped off to laze on a tree branch that hung over the pool.

The air was filled with the soothing sounds of birds twittering and his family splashing in the pool below.

Before long, Little Tiger had drifted off to sleep. He dreamed that he was not a tiger, but a bird twittering in a tree. He spread his feathery wings and leaped into the air…SPLOSH!

Little Tiger suddenly found himself in the water. He was about to scramble to the bank when he realized how wonderfully cool he felt. And how much fun it was to splash!

Now, Little Tiger loves swimming in the pool every day – and he is very clean too!

Where's Barney?

$\mathbf{M}$ia Meerkat always went to sleep with her teddy, Barney, but one bedtime Barney could not be found.

"We have to find him or none of us will sleep, especially Mia," said Mama.

Mama and Papa searched in the sand dunes and hunted in tunnels. They burrowed and rummaged and scoured.

Then Mama spotted Barney – in the paws of a sleeping jackal! "Uh-oh," she gulped. "This could be tricky."

She pulled Barney free, but then the jackal opened his eyes.

"I found that teddy!" he wailed.

Mama threw Barney to Papa and the jackal bounded after him. Papa threw Barney back to Mama and the jackal chased her. Just in the nick of time, they reached their underground home and the jackal skulked off. Panting, Mama went into Mia's bedroom. But Mia wasn't waiting for Barney…She was fast asleep!

In the morning, Mia got a big surprise. Mama and Papa were snoring on her bedroom floor – cuddling Barney!

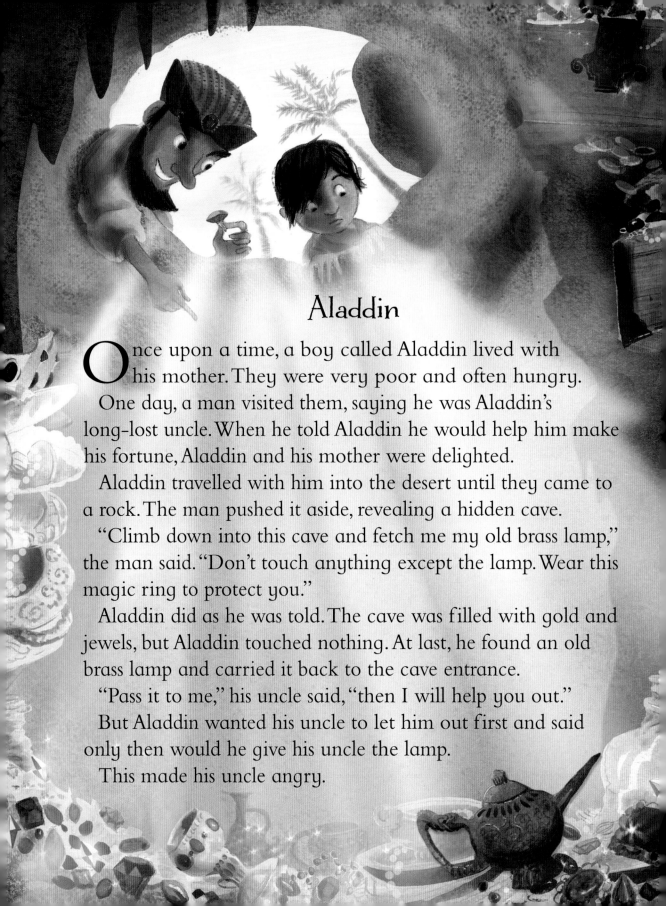

Aladdin

Once upon a time, a boy called Aladdin lived with his mother. They were very poor and often hungry.

One day, a man visited them, saying he was Aladdin's long-lost uncle. When he told Aladdin he would help him make his fortune, Aladdin and his mother were delighted.

Aladdin travelled with him into the desert until they came to a rock. The man pushed it aside, revealing a hidden cave.

"Climb down into this cave and fetch me my old brass lamp," the man said. "Don't touch anything except the lamp. Wear this magic ring to protect you."

Aladdin did as he was told. The cave was filled with gold and jewels, but Aladdin touched nothing. At last, he found an old brass lamp and carried it back to the cave entrance.

"Pass it to me," his uncle said, "then I will help you out."

But Aladdin wanted his uncle to let him out first and said only then would he give his uncle the lamp.

This made his uncle angry.

"Fool!" the man roared, and he rolled the rock back over the cave, trapping Aladdin inside.

"Uncle!" Aladdin cried. "Let me out!"

"I'm not your uncle," said the man. "I'm a sorcerer! Stay there for good if you won't give me the lamp."

As Aladdin wrung his hands in despair, he rubbed the magic ring on his finger.

Suddenly, a genie sprang out and asked, "What do you require, master?"

Astonished, Aladdin asked the genie to take him home. In a flash, Aladdin was outside his mother's house.

Still poor and hungry, Aladdin polished the old lamp, hoping to sell it to get money for food. But as he rubbed the lamp clean, another genie jumped out.

This time, Aladdin asked for food and money, so that he and his mother could live in comfort.

Life went on happily until, one day, Aladdin fell hopelessly in love with the emperor's beautiful daughter. But how could he, Aladdin, marry a princess? Suddenly, he had an idea…He asked the genie of the lamp for gifts to give to the princess.

When the princess thanked Aladdin for the gifts, she fell in love with him. They were soon married and Aladdin asked the genie to build them a beautiful palace.

Hearing that a wealthy stranger had married the princess, the wicked sorcerer guessed that Aladdin must have escaped with the lamp.

One day, when Aladdin was out, the sorcerer disguised himself as a poor tradesman. He stood outside the palace calling out, "New lamps for old! New lamps for old!"

Aladdin's wife gave her husband's old brass lamp to the sorcerer, who snatched it away and rubbed the lamp. He commanded the genie to carry the palace and the princess far away.

"Oh, no!" cried Aladdin, when he discovered his wife and home gone.

Quickly, he rubbed the magic ring to make the genie appear.

"Please bring back my wife and palace!" Aladdin pleaded.

"Sorry, master, I can't!" said the genie. "I am less powerful than the genie of the lamp."

"Then take me to her and I'll win her back!" Aladdin cried.

At once, he found himself in a strange city, but outside his own palace. Through a window, he saw his wife crying and the sorcerer sleeping. Aladdin crept into the palace. He grabbed the magic lamp and rubbed it.

"What do you require, master?" asked the genie.

"Take us straight back home," Aladdin said, "and shut this wicked sorcerer in the cave for a thousand years!"

In a moment, the palace was back where it belonged. With the sorcerer gone, Aladdin and the princess were safe, and they never needed to call on the genie again.

Mermaid's Treasure

One morning, Pearl the mermaid was playing around a reef when she spotted a large sea chest among the coral. She swam closer.

"It must have fallen out of a ship!" she exclaimed. "I wonder what's inside?"

But when she tried to lift the lid, she found that it was locked.

"Oh, bother," Pearl muttered. "Now I want to look inside even more!"

She tried to force the lid open with a clamshell, but it wouldn't budge. So she asked her biggest, strongest friends for help.

Shark tried to bite a hole in it. Octopus wrapped his tentacles around the chest and tried to squeeze it open. Whale tried crushing it with his weight.

"It's no use," sighed Pearl. "We'll never get it open."

"May I try?" said a squeaky voice in her ear.

Pearl turned and saw a tiny shrimp, no bigger than her fingernail. She smiled at him. How could someone so small open the chest?

"Of course you may," she said politely.

The little shrimp wriggled through the keyhole. Pearl, Shark, Octopus and Whale watched as the shrimp reached into the lock with his spindly legs. Then, there was a loud click and the chest unlocked.

The shrimp swam out, looking very pleased with himself.

"Well done!" cried Pearl.

Slowly, she lifted the lid. The chest was full of men's clothes! Pearl sat back and laughed loudly.

"Some poor sailor has lost his luggage," she chuckled. "I suppose it would be treasure to him!"

She looked at her friends and laughed again.

"Don't look so disappointed," she went on. "We may not have gold or jewels, but we've made a very clever friend."

And the little pink shrimp blushed bright red!

Jerry's Sandcastle

Jerry the hamster lived beside the sea. From his cage in the window, he watched children building sandcastles and splashing in the water.

"I wish I could play in the sand," he sighed.

Then, one night, Jerry reached through the bars and unlocked his cage. He slipped out and ran all the way to the beach.

"How wonderful!" he said, gazing at the moonlit sea.

As the waves crashed on the shore, he built turrets and battlements, dungeons and towers. He played in his sandcastle all night. Then, he scurried into the sand dunes and fell fast asleep.

When Jerry woke up, the sea had washed his castle away. He looked up at his cage in the window. He missed the warm house and his cosy cage, and decided to go home. Of course, now he could visit the beach whenever he wanted!

"I can build sandcastles every night," he said. "And my next one will be even bigger!"

A Chilly Change

Edward the polar bear and his brother Charlie sold vanilla ice cream. But Edward had big ideas. He wanted to do something special with the ice cream – something different.

"Maybe I should make up some flavours," he said.

"Ice-cream flavours – that's crazy!" said Charlie. "No one will buy them. Vanilla is best and I don't want to change."

"Change is exciting!" said Edward.

"Change is scary," said Charlie.

But Edward wouldn't give up. He thought about all the tastes he loved. Then he started inventing. Fish and iceberg flavour! Eel surprise! Salt and snowberries! Edward invented a new taste every day.

Edward and Charlie started to sell more and more ice cream. The news spread, and soon seals, gulls and Arctic foxes were queuing up to taste the incredible flavours.

"You were right," Charlie laughed, at last. "I'm sorry. Sometimes, change is a very exciting thing indeed!"

Bunny Loves to Write

One lovely sunny day, Buster Bunny was going out to play in the park with his friends.

"Always carrying a book!" chuckled Mum. "What is it this time, Buster? An adventure? A ghost story?"

"It's not a storybook," smiled Buster. "It's a notebook. My teacher wants everyone in the class to make up a story."

"That sounds fun," said Mum. "What are you going to write?"

"I don't know," said Buster. "I can't think of anything!"

"Oh, you'll have lots of ideas soon," said Mum. "But write them down right away or you'll forget them!"

Buster set off to the park. Soon, he met Francine the frog.

"Lend me a paw with this heavy picnic basket," she said.

"A picnic? It feels more like treasure!" grunted Buster.

Then he took out his notebook. "I've just had my first idea. My story could be about treasure!"

They kept walking toward the park, but soon Francine stopped.

"I'm sure I just saw Max," she said.

"Me too," said Buster, puzzled. "But it looks like he's disappeared."

"As if by magic!" smiled Francine.

"Magic, huh?" said Buster. "Maybe someone could do magic in my story. Like a wizard!"

Suddenly…BOO!

Max the mouse jumped out from a bush.

"Eek! You scared me!" laughed Francine.

"And you've given me another idea," said Buster. "Something scary. There could be spooky ghosts in my story!"

The three friends started crossing a stream near their friend Sam's house when…SPLASH! Buster slipped into the water.

"Phew!" grinned Buster. "At least my notebook didn't get wet! And I've just had another idea. One of the characters could live in the water."

"Like a mermaid," suggested Max.

"Hi, everyone," said Sam. "I'll be ready in a minute. Do you want to come up in the tree and wait?"

"What, up there?" gasped Francine. "No way! You're almost in the sky!"

"Now, there's an idea," said Buster. "There could be planes in my story."

"Or space rockets," said Max.

"Or aliens!" said Francine.

When they got to the park, the friends met Bella, Buster's sister.

"Hi, everyone!" she said. "Hey, Buster, what are you writing?"

"I'm writing a story," said Buster. "I've had lots of ideas and now I'm making them into a real adventure!"

"Cool," said Bella. "Can we hear it?"

"Okay," said Buster. "But it isn't finished yet."

Buster opened his notebook and began to read. "Once upon a time, there were a brother and a sister named Gus and Ella…"

"That's you and me!" giggled Bella.

"They lived in a town next to a friendly wizard," continued Buster. "He let the children play in his haunted castle."

"A wizard! I love stories about magic!" cried Francine.

"Ooh, ghosts! Great!" said Max.

"One day, Gus and Ella found a chest in the attic. They opened the lid. The chest was full of gold!" read Buster. "They had found the lost treasure of Meowlin! But the very next night, the treasure vanished. Where had it gone?"

Buster turned the page and continued, "In the castle moat lived a frog named Fiona, who said aliens from Mars had stolen the treasure! So the wizard waved his wand, and they all flew to Mars by magic!"

Buster stopped reading and sighed, "That's as far as I got."

"We'll help you finish it!" cried Sam.

Everyone took turns writing in Buster's notebook.

"Okay," he said when they were finished. "Here's the rest of the story! I'll read it to you."

"The wizard tricked the aliens and took back the chest. Everyone sneaked into a rocket and escaped. But the aliens followed them and caught them! Then a ghost scared the aliens away for good!" Buster said, as he finished the story.

"Hooray!" everyone cheered.

"There's just one last thing to add," continued Buster. And he wrote:

"*They all lived happily ever after. THE END.*"

Rumpelstiltskin

Long ago, a poor miller was so desperate to impress the king that he told him his daughter could spin straw into gold!

"This I must see," said the king.

The next day, at the palace, the king led the girl to a room filled with straw.

"Spin this into gold by morning," he demanded, then left.

The girl wept at the impossible task. Suddenly, a strange little man appeared.

"Give me your necklace and I will help you," he told her.

The girl handed it to him, and the strange little man sat in front of the spinning wheel and spun the straw into gold.

The next day, the delighted king took the miller's daughter to an even bigger room filled with straw.

"Spin this into gold and you shall be my queen!" he said.

The strange little man appeared once more, but the girl had nothing left to give him.

"If you become queen," he told her, "you can give me your first-born child."

The girl agreed. Once again, he spun the straw into gold.

The next day, the king married the miller's daughter, and the new queen soon forgot all about the strange little man.

A year passed and the queen had a bonny baby boy. It did not take long for the little man to appear again.

"Please don't take my son," the queen begged.

"If you guess my name, you can keep your baby. You have three days," said the little man.

For two nights after that, the little man appeared in the baby's nursery. The queen tried to guess his name, but all of her guesses were wrong.

On the morning of the third day, one of the queen's servants was in the forest chopping logs when he saw a funny little man leaping around a fire and singing. The servant hid behind a tree and listened:

"*The queen will never win my game,*
For Rumpelstiltskin is my name!"

The servant hurried home to tell the queen.

That night, when the queen correctly guessed the little man's name, he was furious. He turned red with rage and ran off into the forest, never to be seen again.

Fairy Friends Forever

Deep in the woods, poor Eloise the fairy was trapped under a nutshell that had fallen from a tree. Try as she might, it was just too heavy for her to move.

Then, suddenly, the nutshell lifted and a little girl gazed down at her.

Eloise was scared of humans, but the girl looked kind.

"Thank you," she said. "What's your name?"

"Matilda," whispered the girl. "Are you really a fairy?"

Eloise had an idea. She waved her wand and shrank Matilda to fairy size.

"Come to Fairyland and find out!" she giggled.

Eloise showed Matilda all around her magical home. They had tea in her toadstool house and gathered dewberries in the Fairyland Forest. They giggled and shared secrets, and soon they felt as if they had always known each other.

Then, it was time for Matilda to go home. Eloise gave her a tiny Fairyland flower.

"I'll never forget you," she whispered.

"And I won't forget you," promised Matilda, as they linked their little fingers together. "Fairy friends forever!"

Winter Snowdrops

One winter's day, a fairy called Snowdrop was sitting in a tree when she heard someone crying. She fluttered down and saw a girl sitting among the tree roots.

"What's wrong, little girl?" Snowdrop asked.

"I can't find any flowers for my mother's birthday," sobbed the girl.

Snowdrop felt sorry for her.

"Fetch me the smoothest pebble you can find," she said. "Then bury it under the tree."

The little girl searched and searched, and finally found a pebble as smooth as silk. She buried it, as she'd been told, and patted the soil down. Then Snowdrop waved her wand, and tiny plant shoots poked through the soil and started to grow. They rose higher and higher, until they burst into brilliant white snowdrops.

"Thank you!" said the little girl, picking the flowers. "Mummy will love them."

The little girl never saw Snowdrop again. But every year, on the girl's mother's birthday, Snowdrop secretly used her magic, and there was always a patch of bright snowdrops waiting for the girl to pick them!

The Little Mermaid

Long ago, a mer-king lived under the sea with his six mermaid daughters, who all sang beautifully.

"When you are twenty-one," he said, "you can go to the surface and see the world above the sea."

One by one, the sisters visited the surface. At last, it was the turn of the youngest sister, and the little mermaid swam eagerly up to the ocean's surface.

On a nearby ship, some people were throwing a party for the handsome prince on board.

As the little mermaid swam closer for a better look, a storm suddenly tossed the ship from side to side and the prince was thrown into the churning water. The little mermaid dived down to rescue him.

Swimming close to the land, she gently pushed the unconscious prince onto the beach. His eyes flickered open and he smiled, before closing them again. As she swam away, the little mermaid saw some people coming down the beach to help him. So she dived beneath the waves and swam home.

The little mermaid told her sisters that she had fallen in love with the prince and longed to see him again.

"I know where his palace is," said her oldest sister. "I'll show you."

After that, the little mermaid swam to the surface every day, hoping to catch a glimpse of the prince.

"Can I become a human?" she asked her father one day.

"Only if a human falls in love with you," said the king gently.

But the little mermaid could not forget the prince. So she visited the sea witch.

"I can make a potion to make you human," hissed the witch. "But I will take your beautiful voice in return. You will only get it back if the prince falls in love with you."

The little mermaid loved the prince so much that she agreed. She swam to the prince's palace and drank the potion. She fell into a deep sleep. When she woke up, she was lying on the beach dressed in beautiful clothes. Where her shiny tail had been, she now had a pair of pale human legs. The little mermaid tried to stand, but her new legs wobbled and she stumbled.

As she fell, two strong arms reached out and caught her. The little mermaid looked up. It was the prince! She tried to speak, but her voice had gone, and she could only smile at her handsome rescuer.

The silent, beautiful stranger fascinated the prince. He grew very fond of her and they spent their afternoons together.

One day, the prince told the little mermaid that he was getting married to a princess.

"My parents want me to do this," he sighed sadly. "But I love another girl. I don't know who she is, but she once rescued me from the sea."

The little mermaid was devastated, but without a voice, how could she tell the prince that she was that girl?

Just before the wedding, the prince walked with the little mermaid along the beach.

"Once I'm married, I won't be able to spend much time with you," he sighed.

The little mermaid nodded sadly. Suddenly, a huge wave crashed over the prince and the little mermaid, washing them out to sea. Without thinking, the little mermaid dived beneath the churning waves and grabbed the prince, taking him back to the shore.

"You're the girl who saved me before!" he cried.

The little mermaid smiled and nodded.

"I can't marry the princess. I love you," he sighed. "Will you marry me?" And as he kissed her, something magical happened. She could feel her voice returning!

"Yes!" she cried out with joy.

The happy couple were married the very next day. The little mermaid's dreams had come true, but she never forgot her family, or that she had once been a mermaid.

129

I Love My Grandma

Little Hedgehog and Grandma Hedgehog loved to play hide and seek together. One day, when Grandma went to find Little Hedgehog to help her make a picnic, he hid behind a bush.

"Where can Little Hedgehog be?" said Grandma.

Little Hedgehog giggled.

"Oh, well. I shall just have to make the picnic myself," said Grandma.

Little Hedgehog followed closely behind Grandma.

"I wish Little Hedgehog were here to help me pick juicy blackberries," said Grandma.

When she wasn't looking, Little Hedgehog picked the biggest blackberries he could reach and put them into Grandma's basket!

"What a lot of berries!" said Grandma, surprised. "I have enough for baking now."

Little Hedgehog scampered into Grandma's kitchen to find the best place to hide. He crouched down low, so that Grandma couldn't see him.

"If only Little Hedgehog were here to help me," said Grandma.

Little Hedgehog licked his lips as Grandma Hedgehog poured sweet, scrumptious honey into her mixing bowl.

When Grandma wasn't looking, Little Hedgehog crept out from his hiding place to taste the honey. Then he quickly hid again.

"Someone has been tasting my honey," said Grandma. "And they have left sticky footprints!"

Grandma followed the teeny-tiny, sticky footprints across the kitchen and out into the garden.

"Someone has been playing hide and seek with me!" she said, smiling.

The sticky footprints went round and round the garden, and stopped by the flowerpots.

"I've found you, Little Hedgehog!" cried Grandma.

But Little Hedgehog wasn't behind the flowerpots! He was…inside one!

"Surprise!" laughed Little Hedgehog.

"Well done, Little Hedgehog," said Grandma. "You're the best at hide and seek. I hope you're hungry, because our picnic is ready!"

"I am hungry," said Little Hedgehog, eagerly looking around the garden. "But where is the picnic?"

Grandma giggled. "You have to find it!" she said.

Little Hedgehog searched around the garden, and soon found honey cookies and fruit salad.

Then, Grandma brought out a giant blackberry cake.

"Yum! I love Grandma's picnics!" Little Hedgehog shouted happily. "And…I love my grandma!"

The Sick Day

Rabbit felt poorly, so his mother wrapped him up in a fluffy blanket and called Dr Hare.

"Maybe he's got a fever," said Dr Hare. "Cool him down with carrot salad."

Rabbit's mother made some carrot salad, but Rabbit wasn't hungry.

"Maybe he's got a cold," said Dr Hare. "Warm him up with carrot soup."

Rabbit's mother cooked up a delicious soup, but Rabbit couldn't even eat a spoonful.

"What do you want, Rabbit?" asked Dr Hare kindly. Rabbit pointed at his mother, who stroked his soft fur and kissed his pink nose. She gave him a big, rabbity cuddle.

"I'm feeling better already," said Rabbit happily.

His mother made him giggle with some funny stories.

By bedtime, Rabbit felt well again. His father came home and Rabbit told him all about the doctor.

"I didn't need salad or soup," he said. "I needed cuddles and funny stories!"

"They're the best medicine of all," said his father wisely.

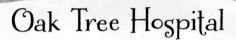

Oak Tree Hospital

One day, Mrs Mouse arrived at Oak Tree Hospital in a fluster. "Please help!" she cried. "My son Luca has a thimble stuck on his head!"

The squirrel nurse tried to pull the thimble off, but Luca yelled, "Ouch!" and "Stop!" so she did. The squirrel doctor smeared Luca's head with honey. It made him very sticky, and got in his eyes and ears, but it didn't move the thimble one bit. Then, the squirrel nurse had a thought.

"Luca, can you waggle your ears and wiggle your eyebrows?" she asked.

Luca waggled and wiggled as hard as he could, while the squirrel nurse and Mrs Mouse and the squirrel doctor tugged on the thimble. And with a loud POP! the thimble flew into the air and hit the squirrel doctor on the nose.

From then on, just in case, Mrs Mouse made Luca practise waggling and wiggling every single day – and kept him well away from thimbles!

Thumbelina

There was once a poor woman who lived alone in a small cottage. She longed to have a child, so one day she visited a fairy to ask for her help.

"You are a kind and good woman," said the fairy, "so I will give you this magic seed. Plant it, water it and you will see what you will see."

The woman thanked the fairy and did as she was told. Soon, a flower bud appeared, with glossy pink petals wrapped tightly around its centre.

"What a beautiful flower you will be," smiled the woman. As she bent to kiss the flower, its petals unfolded, and in the centre was a beautiful girl, the size of a thumb. The woman was overjoyed.

"I will call you Thumbelina," she cried, and she laid her new child in a walnut-shell bed with a rose-petal quilt.

Thumbelina and her mother were very happy. Then, one day, while her mother was away, an ugly, slimy toad crawled into the cottage and took Thumbelina while she slept.

When she woke up, Thumbelina found herself on a lily pad in the middle of a stream, with two warty toads staring at her.

"This is your new wife!" the mother toad told her warty son.

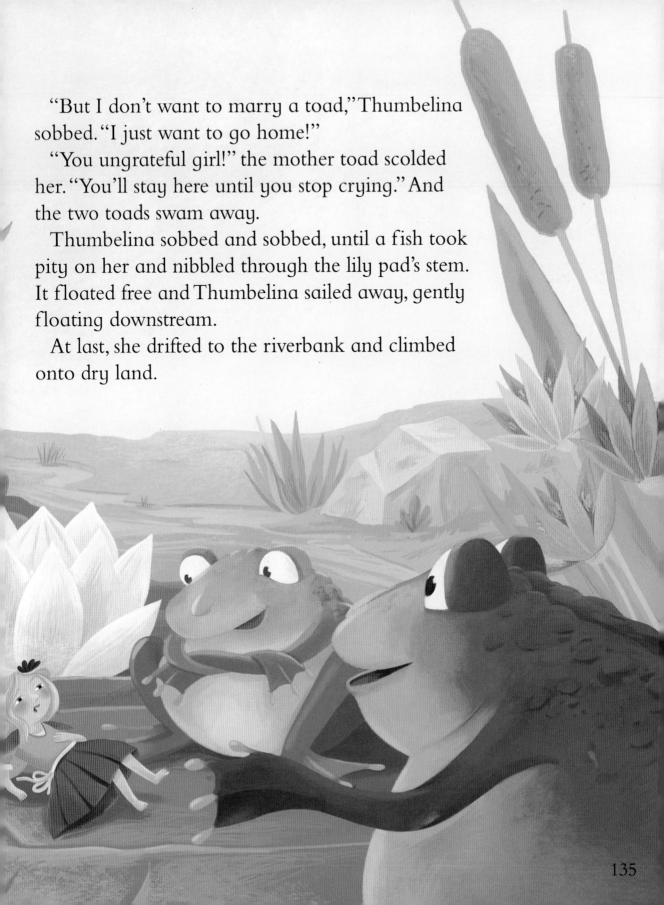

"But I don't want to marry a toad," Thumbelina sobbed. "I just want to go home!"

"You ungrateful girl!" the mother toad scolded her. "You'll stay here until you stop crying." And the two toads swam away.

Thumbelina sobbed and sobbed, until a fish took pity on her and nibbled through the lily pad's stem. It floated free and Thumbelina sailed away, gently floating downstream.

At last, she drifted to the riverbank and climbed onto dry land.

All that summer, Thumbelina lived in the countryside. She missed her mother terribly, but she busied herself making friends with the birds and small creatures she met.

Then winter came. Thumbelina was cold and hungry. Luckily, a kindly field mouse invited her to stay with him in his burrow. She was so grateful that she said yes at once.

Life underground was warm and snug, but Thumbelina missed the sunshine. And then Mouse's friend Mole asked her to marry him.

"But I don't want to marry a mole," cried Thumbelina.

"You ungrateful girl!" said the mouse. So Thumbelina sadly agreed to marry the mole and a date was set for the following summer.

Thumbelina was miserable. Then, one day, as she walked through the underground tunnels, she found a swallow, almost dead with the cold. She hugged the bird against herself to warm him. He slowly opened his eyes.

"You have saved my life," said the swallow. "Come with me to the south, to the land of sunshine and flowers."

"I cannot leave Mouse," sighed Thumbelina. "He has been so kind to me."

"Then I must go alone," said the swallow. "But I will return next summer. Goodbye!" And he flew away.

Finally, the day Thumbelina had been dreading arrived – the day she would marry Mole. As she waited for Mole to arrive, the swallow appeared again.

"Come with me now!" he cried.

This time, Thumbelina said, "I will!"

So Thumbelina flew away to the south with the swallow, to a land full of flowers. As she bent to smell one especially beautiful flower, the petals opened, and there in the centre was a fairy prince, no bigger than a thumb, with butterfly wings.

"Will you be my wife?" he asked at once.

"I will!" cried Thumbelina.

So Thumbelina married the fairy prince and became queen of the flower fairies. She did not forget her dear mother and arranged for fairy messengers to deliver a letter to her, along with a bouquet of beautiful flowers.

Thumbelina and her handsome prince lived happily ever after.

Flamingo's Dance Class

Flamingo was a very elegant bird. She never tripped over or bumped into things. But the other animals in the jungle weren't always so graceful.

"Look out!" Flamingo exclaimed as Elephant barged into a tree.

"Be careful!" she cried when Hippo wiped mud on her feathers.

"Watch your step!" she squeaked as Crocodile trampled over her toes. "You're all so clumsy!"

Elephant, Hippo and Crocodile felt embarrassed. They didn't want the other animals to think they were clumsy.

"A ballet lesson will help," said Flamingo.

First, she showed her class how to do a pirouette.

"Now it's your turn," she said.

Elephant did her best, but she was so heavy that she just drilled a hole deep into the ground and got her leg stuck.

"Perhaps a pirouette is too hard," said Flamingo. "Try this instead."

She stood on one leg in a beautiful pose and tucked the other leg under her body. Hippo tried to copy her, but he accidentally kicked a tree and knocked it down. Flamingo groaned.

"Perhaps you would be more graceful if you looked prettier," she said, handing them some tutus. "Try these on."

But poor Crocodile's belly was so low to the ground that his tutu dragged in the mud.

"I don't think we'll ever be as elegant as you, Flamingo," said Elephant sadly.

Flamingo sighed and looked at her friends. Elephant could use her trunk to pick leaves and berries gently. Hippo dived underwater without bumping into anything, and when Crocodile glided into the swamp, he didn't make a single ripple.

Suddenly, Flamingo felt very silly. Why was she trying to change her friends? When they acted naturally, they all looked graceful.

"I'm sorry I called you clumsy," she said. "You're perfect just the way you are!"

The Biggest Squeak in the World

Freddie couldn't squeak. Squeaking doesn't matter if you're a dog or a cat, but unfortunately Freddie was a mouse. And mice are supposed to squeak.

"All my friends can squeak," he said. "What's wrong with me?"

"You're just not ready yet," said his grandfather. "It will happen when the time is right."

Later that day, Freddie was moping outside the mouse hole when suddenly…HISS! A huge, hungry cat came springing towards him!

Freddie opened his mouth to yell for help – and instead let out an enormous SQUEAK! Every single mouse in the town heard it. Dogs heard it. Even humans heard it. The cat leaped into the air and all its fur stood on end. Then it shot away in terror.

When the other mice heard about the cat, they gave Freddie a big cheer.

"That's why your squeak took a long time to come," his grandfather laughed. "It's the biggest squeak in the world!"

Curious Kitten

Misty was a curious kitten. One day, she was watching Mrs Duck lead her waddling ducklings across the yard.

"I wonder what it's like being a duck," she thought.

She scurried along behind the ducklings, trying her best to quack, but all she could manage was a strange "Meow-ack!"

When the ducklings nibbled the grass on the riverbank, Misty tried a little herself, but it made her cough.

Then, the ducklings followed their mother into the lake for a swim.

"That looks easy," cried Misty, and she jumped in with a big SPLASH! But swimming wasn't at all easy for a kitten!

Luckily, Scratch the sheepdog was nearby. He leaped in and gently pulled Misty out, using his teeth on the scruff of her neck.

"Thanks," said Misty. "I thought it would be fun to be a duck, but I think I'll stick to being a kitten."

She had just sat down to lick her fur dry when she had an idea – perhaps she could try being a sheepdog instead!

The Elves and the Shoemaker

There was once a poor shoemaker who lived with his wife. "We only have enough leather to make one more pair of shoes to sell," said the shoemaker.

So he cut out the leather, ready to stitch the next day, then went to bed.

That night, two elves crept into the shop, dressed in rags. They found the leather and set to work.

The next morning, the shoemaker was amazed to find the finest pair of shoes he had ever seen.

A rich gentleman saw the stylish shoes in the shop and tried them on. He was so delighted with the fit that he paid the shoemaker twice the asking price.

"We can buy more leather," the shoemaker told his wife.

That evening, the shoemaker cut out two more pairs of shoes from the leather, then went to bed.

During the night, the two elves crept into the shop again and set to work on the leather.

In the morning, the shoemaker found two pairs of beautiful shoes. He sold them for more money than he had ever thought possible. Now, the shoemaker had enough money to make four new pairs of shoes.

"Who is helping us?" asked the shoemaker's wife.

That night, the shoemaker cut out the new leather, then he and his wife hid and waited.

It wasn't long before the two little elves appeared and set to work on the leather.

"We must repay our little helpers for their kindness," the shoemaker told his wife.

"Let's make them some fine clothes," said his wife.

So they made the elves two little pairs of trousers, two smart coats and two warm, woolly scarves.

That night, the shoemaker and his wife hid again and watched as the elves found their tiny outfits! They quickly dressed, then danced away happily into the night.

The shoemaker and his wife never saw the elves again. But they continued to make fine shoes and were never poor.

The Boy Who Cried Wolf

Once there was a boy called Peter who lived in a little village in the mountains with his parents, who were sheep farmers. It was Peter's job to watch over the flock and protect the sheep from wolves.

Every day, Peter sat on the mountainside watching the flock. It was very quiet with no one but sheep for company. No wolves ever came to eat the sheep.

"Oh, I wish something exciting would happen," groaned Peter. "I'm so bored!"

Finally, one day, Peter couldn't stand it any more. He started shouting at the top of his voice, "WOLF! HELP! WOLF!"

Down in the village, a man heard Peter's cries.

"Quick!" he shouted. "There's a wolf attacking the sheep!"

The villagers grabbed their axes, forks and shovels, and ran up the mountain to where Peter was shepherding his flock.

When they got there, the sheep were grazing peacefully.

"Where's the wolf?" one of the villagers cried.

Peter roared with laughter. "There's no wolf. I was just playing!"

The villagers were very angry. "You mustn't cry wolf when there isn't one," they said.

That night, Peter got a telling-off from his mother and was sent to bed without any supper.

For a while after this, Peter managed to behave himself, and the villagers soon forgot about his trick.

Then, one day, Peter was bored again. Laughing, he picked up some sticks and started banging them hard together. Then at the top of his voice, he shouted, "WOLF! HELP! WOLF! There's a big wolf eating the sheep!"

Down in the village, a crowd of people started gathering when they heard the loud banging and shouting.

"It's Peter," someone cried. "Quick, there must be a wolf on the prowl!"

Once again, the villagers grabbed their axes, forks and shovels. They ran up the mountain to chase away the wolf, and save poor Peter and his sheep.

And once again, when they got there,
the sheep were grazing peacefully.

"Peter, what's happened?" shouted
one man angrily.

"There's no wolf," laughed Peter.
"I was only playing."

"You shouldn't do that," said another man. "It's not
good to lie."

That night, Peter got an even bigger telling-off from
his mother and once again had to go to bed without
any supper.

Peter decided that he would really try to behave himself
from now on and soon the incident was forgotten.

A few weeks later, while Peter stood counting the
sheep to pass the time, he noticed that some
of them were bleating nervously.

He climbed up a tree to see what
was upsetting them.

To his horror, he saw a big wolf creeping through the grass towards the flock.

Shaking with fear, he started screaming, "WOLF! HELP! WOLF! Please hurry, there's a big wolf about to eat the sheep!"

A few people down in the village heard his cries for help, but they carried on about their business as usual.

"It's only Peter playing another trick," they said to each other. "Does he think he can fool us again?"

And so nobody went to Peter's rescue.

By nightfall, when Peter hadn't returned, his parents became concerned. Peter never missed his supper – something bad must have happened.

The villagers hurried up the mountain, carrying flaming torches to light their way.

A terrible sight met their eyes. All the sheep were gone! There really had been a wolf this time.

Peter was still in the tree, shaking and crying.

"I cried out wolf! Why didn't you come?" he wept.

"Nobody believes a liar, even when he's speaking the truth," said Peter's father, helping him climb out of the tree. Peter hung on to his father all the way home. He never wanted to see another wolf ever again.

And Peter finally really learned his lesson. He never told a lie again and he always got to eat his dinner.

I Won't Budge!

T he animals were hot and bothered. There had been no rain for days and the watering hole was beginning to dry up under the hot African sun.

"Let's take turns cooling down in the water," suggested the antelope, and all the other animals agreed.

But when the hippo took his turn, he refused to come out of the water.

"You're not being fair," shouted the other animals. "We all want a go."

"No way," said the hippo. "It's far too nice in here. I WON'T BUDGE!"

"That's so mean!" cried the animals. "Please let us have a turn."

But the selfish hippo just chanted, "I WON'T BUDGE! I WON'T BUDGE!"

As the sun grew hotter, more animals came to the watering hole. Still the hippo wouldn't budge.

Suddenly, a thundering noise boomed across the plains, followed by a huge thirsty elephant heading right for the watering hole!

All the animals fled, including the hippo, as the elephant charged into the water. SPLASH!

Once the elephant was settled, the other animals returned.

"Now the elephant won't budge," the hippo grunted.

"Well, you did the same to us," huffed the antelope.

The elephant heard this conversation and felt sorry for the sweltering animals. Then he had an idea.

"One…two…three…SQUIRT!" trumpeted the elephant.

"Aaaaah!" sighed the animals, as the spray cooled them down.

But the hippo had been left out.

"Hey, can I have some?" he asked.

"No," said the elephant. "Now you know how it feels."

The hippo drooped his head in shame and turned away.

After a few minutes, the huge elephant shouted, "I think you've learned your lesson."

He grinned at the other animals and cried, "One…two…three…SQUIRT!"

"Thank you!" sighed the hippo, as the cool water splashed against his hot skin. "I won't budge from HERE now!"

Can Ladybirds Change their Spots?

Mabel the ladybird and her friend Archie loved setting each other challenges. And the harder they were, the better Mabel and Archie liked them.

"I challenge you to change your spots," said Archie one morning.

"That's impossible!" said Mabel.

But Archie just laughed. So Mabel thought hard, and then she had an idea. She flew all around the garden and collected colourful petals and tiny patterned leaves. Then she used threads of grass to attach the decorations to her wings. When she flew back to Archie, she was covered with splodges and stripes of yellow and blue, and pink and purple.

"Who are you?" Archie gasped. "I've never seen a bug like you before!"

"It's me!" giggled Mabel.

Archie giggled too. He tried on some of the petals and leaves, and they played dressing-up till bedtime.

"Tomorrow it's my turn to think of a challenge!" said Mabel. "I can't wait!"

What Ghosts Like Best

The friendliest ghost in the fairground was called Milo and he loved telling jokes.

"Do humans like jokes?" he asked the other ghosts.

"Don't ask silly questions," they said. "Humans hate jokes."

One day, a sad-looking boy called William got on the ghost train. Milo sat next to him.

"Hello," he said. "Do you like jokes?"

William looked scared, but Milo thought he'd try a joke anyway.

"What do ghosts eat?" Milo asked. "Spook-hetti!"

He felt pleased when William giggled.

"What do you call a train with a cold?" he went on. "Achoo choo train!"

William giggled again. All the way around the ride, Milo told jokes and William laughed.

"Is it okay if I come back tomorrow?" asked William at the end of the ride. "I've never laughed so much in my life!"

Milo grinned. "Of course," he said. "And now I know that humans definitely do like jokes!"

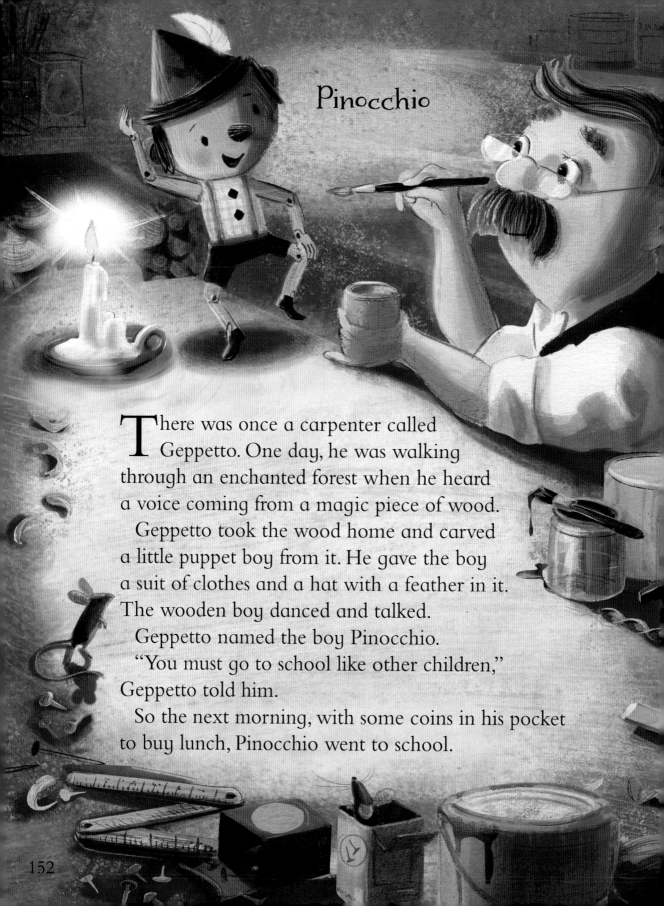

Pinocchio

There was once a carpenter called
Geppetto. One day, he was walking
through an enchanted forest when he heard
a voice coming from a magic piece of wood.

Geppetto took the wood home and carved
a little puppet boy from it. He gave the boy
a suit of clothes and a hat with a feather in it.
The wooden boy danced and talked.

Geppetto named the boy Pinocchio.

"You must go to school like other children,"
Geppetto told him.

So the next morning, with some coins in his pocket
to buy lunch, Pinocchio went to school.

Along the way, a cricket hopped up onto his shoulder.

"You look like you could use a friend," he told Pinocchio. "I will help you learn right from wrong."

Further down the road, Pinocchio met a fox and a cat. They had heard his money jangling in his pocket.

"Come and play with us!" said the fox slyly.

"Pinocchio, you promised your father you would go to school," the cricket whispered.

But Pinocchio, not knowing any better, followed the cat and the fox into a dark forest.

"Plant your money here and it will grow into a money tree," they told Pinocchio. "Just come back tomorrow and you'll see."

The next morning, instead of going to school, Pinocchio went to find his money tree. But when he reached the spot where he'd buried his coins, there was no money tree and his coins had gone.

"They played a trick on you," sighed his friend, the cricket. "They just wanted to get your money."

Pinocchio felt silly, but he pretended he didn't care and stomped off into the forest. The little cricket begged him to go back to Geppetto, but Pinocchio wouldn't listen. Just as it was getting dark, they came to a tiny cottage. Pinocchio knocked on the door loudly and a pretty fairy answered.

"We're lost," explained Pinocchio. "Please can you help us?"

The fairy invited them in and gave them some food.
"Why are you so far from home?" she asked kindly.
Pinocchio didn't want to tell her that he had disobeyed his father.
"I was chased by a giant!" he lied.
Suddenly, Pinocchio's nose grew a little.
"And I ran into the forest to escape!" he continued.
And Pinocchio's nose grew again!
"I have put a spell on you!" said the fairy. "Every time you tell a lie, your wooden nose will grow."
Pinocchio began to cry. "I won't tell any more lies," he promised.
The fairy waved her wand and Pinocchio's nose returned to normal.
"From now on, I will do just as Father tells me," he said. But when he returned home, Geppetto wasn't there. He was out searching for Pinocchio!
"We must find Father and bring him home," he sobbed, feeling bad.
They began their search by the river. But when they got there, Pinocchio fell into the water. The cricket jumped in to help him, but an enormous fish swallowed them both.
There, in the fish's tummy, they found Geppetto! He had been swallowed by the fish too.

Pinocchio hugged his father tightly. "I won't leave you again!" he said.

Then, Pinocchio took the feather from his hat and tickled the fish.

"A...a...a...choo!" The fish gave a mighty sneeze, and Geppetto, Pinocchio and the cricket flew out of the fish's mouth and landed on the riverbank.

That night, as Pinocchio slept in his own little bed, the kind fairy flew in through his window.

"You're a good, brave boy," she said, and she kissed him on the forehead.

When Pinocchio awoke the next morning, he found that he was no longer made from wood. He was a real boy! From then on he was always a good son to Geppetto and the best of friends with the cricket, who didn't need to tell him right from wrong ever again.

I Love My Grandpa

One sunny afternoon, Little Bear went for a walk by the river with Grandpa Bear.

"Shall we have a paddle, Little Bear?"

Little Bear shook his head. "I don't like water, Grandpa," he said.

"Let's just put one paw in," said Grandpa, "and see what it feels like."

Grandpa Bear put one paw in the water.

"Ah!" he said. "That feels good!"

Little Bear put only the tip of his paw in. Then he giggled.

"The water tickles!" he said, and he put the rest of his paw in and waved it about. "Wheeee!"

Grandpa Bear put two paws in. So did Little Bear.

Then Little Bear put all four of his little paws into the cool water.

"Well done, Little Bear!" said Grandpa. "You're paddling! Now, are you ready to make a splash?"

Little Bear kicked his feet, making splashes with a swoosh-swoosh-swoosh! Then suddenly…

SPLOOSH!

In jumped Grandpa Bear, making a gigantic splash!

"Yippee!" cried Little Bear.

"Shall we have a swim now, Little Bear?" said Grandpa Bear.

Little Bear shook his head. "I can't swim, Grandpa!" he said.

"Let's just float," said Grandpa, "and see what it feels like. I will hold you."

When Little Bear felt his grandpa holding him,
he lifted up one paw at a time, until…

"You're floating!" said Grandpa Bear. "Now, how
about some more splashing?"

Little Bear kicked his feet, making more swoosh-swooshes!
And suddenly…

"You're swimming, Little Bear!" said Grandpa.

Little Bear swam around and around his grandpa.

"You're the best little swimmer there is," said Grandpa
Bear proudly.

When it was time to get out, Grandpa Bear helped Little
Bear climb out of the water. Then they both wriggled and
jiggled to get dry, spraying water all about.

Grandpa Bear gave Little Bear a warming hug.

"Do you like water now, Little Bear?" he asked, smiling.

Little Bear grinned. "I love water!" he shouted happily.
"And…I love my grandpa!"

The Pink Princess

Princess Sophia loved pink. She had a bright pink room with a plump pink bed. She had a huge pink wardrobe full of frilly pink dresses. She had rosebud-pink shoes and a pink tiara.

One day, Princess Chloe came to play at the palace. She brought Princess Sophia a lovely new necklace! But there was only one problem…

"It's not pink!" cried Princess Sophia. It really was beautiful, but it wouldn't go with her pink dress, pink shoes or pink tiara!

"Let's go and play!" cried Princess Chloe.

Princess Sophia put the necklace in her pocket and followed Princess Chloe into the palace garden.

Princess Chloe ran up to the gardener, who was busy mowing the palace lawn.

"May we pick some flowers, please?" asked Princess Chloe.

When the gardener said that they could, Princess Chloe skipped away, picking different-coloured flowers as she went.

Princess Sophia noticed some bright purple blossom. She picked some of it and put it in her hair, just like Princess Chloe.

Princess Chloe started to climb a huge tree.

"Princesses don't climb trees!" gasped Princess Sophia.

"Why not?" said Princess Chloe. "Look, I've found some ribbons up here!"

Princess Sophia recognized the ribbons of a kite she had lost. She climbed up into the tree. Princess Chloe untangled the ribbons and tied one around each of their waists.

"Now catch me if you can!" said Princess Chloe, and she scrambled down the tree and ran to the pond.

A dragonfly fluttered past them, its shimmering wings catching the sun. It landed on Princess Chloe's outstretched hand. Princess Sophia jumped back nervously.

Princess Chloe whispered to the dragonfly, "She doesn't like anything that isn't pink."

"Yes, I do!" shouted Princess Sophia. "I like the bright flowers and the rainbow-coloured ribbons, and the blue pond and this gorgeous, multi-coloured dragonfly!"

"Why don't you try on your new necklace now?" asked Princess Chloe.

Princess Sophia admired her colourful reflection in the pond.

"I don't mind that it's not a pink necklace," she said, smiling. "Because I'm not just a pink princess any more!"

Dillon the Digger's Challenge

It was Dillon the digger's first day on the building site and he was nervous. He had to dig twenty holes for posts to go in. It was the biggest job Dillon had ever done and the other machines didn't seem very friendly at first.

"You're very little," grumbled the cement mixer.

"I hope you're a fast worker," said the crane.

"I'll try my best," Dillon whispered.

Dillon dug and scooped and shovelled. Faster and faster! Then the crane lifted the posts into place and the mixer poured in the concrete. At last, the job was finished, right at the end of the day.

"You might be small, but you're speedy," said the crane, as they settled down for the night.

"Welcome to the team!" added the mixer.

Dillon felt tired, but proud. It was good to be needed and he couldn't wait for another busy day of digging!